SOVIET LITERATURE FOR YOUNG PEOPLE

Alexei Tolstoi

NIKITA'S CHILDHOOD

Fredonia Books
Amsterdam, The Netherlands

Nikita's Childhood

by
Alexei Tolstoi

ISBN: 1-58963-454-3

Fredonia Books
Amsterdam, The Netherlands
http://www.fredoniabooks.com

CONTENTS

SUNNY MORN

Nikita sighed as he awoke and opened his eyes. Through the frosty facework on the windows, through the miraculously painted silver stars and the strange arms of the foliage came the rays of the sun. Inside the room the light was snow-white. The sun was reflected from the wash-basin in a trembling patch of light on the wall.

As he opened his eyes Nikita remembered that the evening before Pakhom the carpenter had said to him:

"Now I'll smear it and pour water over it and when you get up in the morning you can get aboard and off you go."

The evening before Pakhom, a one-eyed, pockmarked peasant, had made a sled for Nikita at the latter's special request. The sled was made like this.

Standing amidst the curling shavings beside the carpenter's bench in the coach-house, Pakhom had planed down two boards and four

legs: the lower board was bevelled at the leading edge so that it would not bite into the snow; the legs were thinned down at the bottom; in the upper board there were two depressions on the edges for the legs so that the rider could keep his seat. The lower board was smeared with cow dung and then water was poured over it as it stood out in the frost, the operation being repeated three times; after this the surface was like that of a mirror. A rope was fixed to the upper board to pull the sled by and to steer it with when racing downhill.

The sled would, of course, now be ready and standing at the door. Pakhom was that sort of chap: "If," he would say, "I promise something, my word's as good as law, and I do it."

Nikita sat on the edge of his bed and listened —the house was quiet, nobody, apparently, was up and about yet. If he could dress himself in a minute, naturally without washing or cleaning his teeth, then he would be able to slip out of the back-door into the yard. And from the yard it was a stone's throw to the river where the snowdrifts piled up against the steep bank—get on the sled and off. . . .

Nikita slipped off the bed and walked on tiptoe across the sun-warmed squares of the floor.

Just then the door opened and a head with glasses, protruding red eyebrows and a bright red beard looked in. The head winked and said:

"Are you getting up, you young brigand?"

ARKADY IVANOVICH

The man with the red beard—he was Nikita's tutor, Arkady Ivano-vich—had been sniffing around since the previous evening and had deliberately got up early. That Arkady Ivanovich was a very smart and cunning fellow. He came into Nikita's room with a knowing smile on his face, went to the window, breathed on the glass and when the frost had melted and the glass was clear, he adjusted his glasses and looked out into the yard.

"There's a fine sled," he said, "standing by the porch."

Nikita did not speak, he only frowned. He had to dress and clean his teeth and wash his face, ears and all, and even his neck. After that Arkady Ivanovich took Nikita by the shoulders and marched him into the dining-room. His mother, in a thick grey dress, was seated at the samovar. She took hold of Nikita's face, with her clear, bright eyes looked into his, and kissed him.

"Did you sleep well, Nikita?"

Then she stretched out her hand to Arkady Ivanovich.

"And how did you sleep, Arkady Ivanovich?" she asked affably.

"As far as sleeping's concerned, well, I slept all right," he answered and laughed into his red moustache for no apparent reason; he sat down to table, poured cream into his tea, took a piece of sugar and placed it between his white teeth and winked at Nikita through his glasses.

Arkady Ivanovich was simply unbearable: he was always jolly, always winking, never said anything straight out, but always left you guessing. For instance when Mamma asked quite plainly how he had slept he answered: "As far as sleeping's concerned, well, I slept all right"—from which it was to be understood: "And Nikita wanted to run away from breakfast and lessons to the river, and yesterday Nikita instead of doing his German translation sat on Pakhom's bench for two hours."

Arkady Ivanovich never made complaints, it is true, but Nikita always had to keep his ears open.

At breakfast Mamma said that there had been a heavy frost during the night and that the water barrel in the passage was frozen and that when Nikita went out he was to wear his Cossack hood.

"But, Mamma, honestly, it's terribly hot," said Nikita.

"Please put on the hood."

"It tickles my cheeks and it stifles me, Mamma, I'll catch a worse cold in the hood."

Mamma looked at Arkady Ivanovich and at Nikita, and when she spoke her voice trembled.

"You're so disobedient, I don't know whom you take after."

"Let's get to our lessons," said Arkady Ivanovich, rubbing his hands as though there were no greater pleasure in the world than solving problems in arithmetic and dictating proverbs and sayings that sent you to sleep.

In the big, empty, white room, with a map of the two hemispheres hanging from the wall, Nikita sat down at a table that was covered

10

with ink-stains and drawings of ugly faces, and Arkady Ivanovich opened the arithmetic book.

"Where did we get to?" he said briskly. With a finely pointed pencil he marked the number of the problem.

"A merchant sold several yards of blue cloth at 3 rubles 64 kopeks a yard and some black cloth," read Nikita. Immediately, as was usually the case, he imagined that merchant from the arithmetic book. He was in a long, dusty frock-coat, had a sour-looking sallow face—a dull, flat and dried-up man. The shop was as dark as a cave; on a dusty flat shelf lay two pieces of cloth; the merchant stretched out his skinny hands, took the cloth from the shelf and looked at Nikita with dull, lifeless eyes.

"Well, what do you think, Nikita?" asked Arkady Ivanovich. "Altogether the merchant sold 18 yards. How much blue cloth and how much black did he sell?"

Nikita frowned, the merchant was squashed flat, the two pieces of cloth disappeared in the wall and rolled up in the dust....

"Ai-ai-ai," said Arkady Ivanovich and began to explain, wrote some figures rapidly with his pencil, multiplied and divided, repeating to himself, "Carry one, carry two." It seemed to Nikita that during multiplication this "Carry one," or "Carry two," jumped up from the paper into his head and tickled his brain so that he would not forget them. It gave a very unpleasant feeling. And the sun that was sparkling on the two frost-bound windows of the class-room was calling all the time: "Come to the river."

At last the arithmetic lesson was finished and the dictation began. Arkady Ivanovich walked up and down along the wall and in a special sleepy sort of voice, a voice that nobody ever uses for speaking, began his dictation:

"All the animals on earth are constantly at labour, working. The pupil was obedient and industrious...."

Sticking out the tip of his tongue Nikita began to write, the pen scratched and splashed.

Suddenly a door slammed somewhere in the house and he could hear the sound of frozen felt boots going down the passage. Arkady Ivanovich lowered his book and listened. Mamma's merry voice exclaimed not very far away:

"Have you brought the mail?"

Nikita dropped his head right into his exercise-book, suppressing his laughter.

"Obedient and industrious," he repeated in a singsong voice. "I've written 'industrious.'"

Arkady Ivanovich adjusted his glasses.

"Hm-m, All the animals on earth are obedient and industrious.... What are you laughing at? Made a blot? By the way, we'll have a short rest now."

Arkady Ivanovich, pressing his lips together, menaced him with a long forefinger that looked like a pencil and went rapidly out of the class-room. In the passage he spoke to Mamma:

"Alexandra Leontievna, is there a letter for me?"

Nikita guessed whom he expected a letter from. There was, however, no time to waste. Nikita put on a short sheepskin jacket, felt boots and cap, threw the hood behind the chest of drawers so that it would not be found and ran out to the porch.

SNOWDRIFTS

The extensive yard was covered with soft, white, scintillating snow broken by deep blue human footprints and the frequent tracks of a dog. The air was brisk and frosty, tickled his nose and pricked his cheeks like needles. The coach-house, sheds and farm-yard wore heavy white caps and seemed to be closer to the earth as though they had grown into the snow. The tracks left by sleigh runners ran like two strips of glass across the whole yard.

Nikita ran down the crunchy steps from the porch. At the bottom stood a brand-new pinewood sled with a coil of bast rope on it. Nikita looked at it—it was solidly made, he tried it—it slid easily; he slung the sled over his shoulder, took up a spade which he thought he might need and ran down the path the whole length of the garden to the dam. There stood huge willow-trees—they reached almost to the sky—all laden with hoar-frost so that each branch looked as though it were made of snow.

Nikita turned to the right, towards the river, and tried to keep to the road, walking in other people's footprints and in places where the snow was untrampled going backwards in order to deceive Arkady Ivanovich.

On the steep banks of the Chagry River huge fluffy snowdrifts had piled up during the past few days. In some places they formed promontories that overhung the river. If you stood on one of these promontories the snow would pull away, collapse and the whole snow mountain would go tumbling down in a cloud of white powder.

To the right the river wound away like a dark blue shadow between white, deserted fields. To the left, on the slope of the high bank, stood the dark cottages of the village of Sosnovka, the long poles over the wells sticking up between them. Watts of blue smoke rose high above the roofs and melted in the air. On the snowy cliff, marred with yellow patches of ash that the housewives had raked out of their stoves that morning, a number of tiny figures were moving. These were Nikita's pals, the small boys from "our end" of the village. Farther on, where the river bent away, there were more boys, the Konchan crowd, a dangerous gang. Nikita threw down the spade, dropped the sled on to the snow, sat on the seat, took a firm hold of the rope, kicked off with his feet a couple of times—and the sled flew away downhill of its own volition. The wind whistled in his ears and powdered snow rose in clouds on either side of him. Down, down he went, swift as an arrow. Quite suddenly, where the snow came to an end over the river, the sled flew into the air and landed on the ice. Gradually it slowed down and then came to a stop.

Nikita laughed, climbed off the sled and dragged it up the hill, up to his knees in snow. When he reached the bank he saw the black figure of Arkady Ivanovich, looking bigger than life size, coming across the white field. Nikita grabbed the spade, jumped on the sled, flew down the bank and then ran across the ice to where the snowdrifts overhang the river.

At the snow cape Nikita immediately began to dig a cave—it was an easy job for the spade cut the snow like butter. When he had a big enough hole, he dragged the sled inside and from within began filling up the entrance with lumps of snow. When the wall was built right up there was a faint blue light inside the cave and it was very pleasant and comfortable.

Nikita sat and thought that not one of the boys had such a wonderful sled. He got out his penknife and began to carve a name on the upper board—"Vevit."

"Nikita! Where have you got to?" he heard Arkady Ivanovich's voice.

Nikita put his knife back in his pocket and looked out through a chink between the lumps of snow. Below him Arkady Ivanovich stood on the ice peering round.

"Where are you, you young brigand?"

Arkady Ivanovich adjusted his glasses and came towards the cave but immediately sank into the snow up to his waist.

"Come on out, I'll drag you out, anyway!"

Nikita did not answer, Arkady Ivanovich tried to climb higher but again sank into the snow; he put his hands in his pockets and said:

"If you don't want to, then you needn't. Stay where you are. Your mother has just got a letter from Samara.... All right, good-bye, I'm going back."

"What letter?" asked Nikita.

"Ah, so you are here!"

"Tell me who the letter was from?"

"About some people coming for the holidays."

Lumps of snow immediately began to fly and Nikita's head appeared out of the cave. Arkady Ivanovich laughed heartily.

THE MYSTERIOUS LETTER

Mother read the letter at last while they were at lunch. The letter was from his father.

"Dear Sasha, I have bought the thing we decided to present to a certain boy who in my opinion hardly deserves to have such nice things given to him." On hearing these words Arkady Ivanovich began winking violently. "It is quite a big present so send an extra sleigh for it. There's another piece of news—Anna Apollosovna Babkina intends to come to us for the holidays with her children...."

"There's nothing more of interest," said Mamma and in answer to all Nikita's questions simply closed her eyes and said:

"I don't know anything."

Arkady Ivanovich also kept silent, waved his hands and said he didn't know anything. In general Arkady Ivanovich was excessively happy that whole day, absent-mindedly gave wrong answers, and kept pulling a note out of his pocket, reading a few lines and screwing up his mouth. Apparently he had a secret of his own.

At dusk Nikita ran across the yard to the workers' quarters where two frozen windows cast a pale blue light on the snow. The workers were at supper. Nikita whistled three times. A minute later his closest friend, Mishka Koryashonok, came out wearing enormous felt boots and no cap and a sheepskin jacket thrown over his shoulders. Behind the corner of the building Nikita told him in a whisper about the letter and asked him what they were bringing from town.

Mishka Koryashonok, his teeth chattering from the cold, said:

"Something awfully big, burst my eyes. I'm running back, it's cold. Listen, we're going to beat up the Konchan gang in the village to-morrow. Coming?"

"All right."

Nikita went back home and sat down to read *The Headless Horseman.*

Mamma and Arkady Ivanovich sat at the round table under the big lamp, each with a book. A cricket was chirping—trr-trr-trr—behind a big stove. The floor boards in the next room creaked in the dark.

The Headless Horseman galloped across the prairie, brushing aside the high grass; a red moon rose over the lake. Nikita felt that the hair on the back of his neck was twitching. He turned round warily—a greyish shadow passed across the black window. Honestly, he saw it. Mamma raised her head from her book.

"The wind has risen this evening, there'll be a blizzard."

THE DREAM

Nikita had a dream—he had dreamed it several times and it was always the same.

Easily and soundlessly the door of the drawing-room opened. On the floor lay the bluish reflections of the windows. Outside the black windows hung the moon—a huge ball of light. Nikita climbed on to the card-table that stood between the two windows and this is what he saw.

On the opposite wall, white as chalk, the round pendulum swaying back and forth in a tall clock-case was gleaming in the darkness. On the wall above the clock hung the framed portrait of a stern-looking old man with a pipe, beside him an old woman in cap and shawl—she looked down with tightly pressed lips. Along the wall, from the clock to the corner, four striped armchairs, their arms outstretched, squatted each on its four legs. A low bandy-legged sofa stood huddled in the corner. They sat there, without faces or eyes staring at the moon, not stirring a bit.

A cat crawled out from under the fringe of the sofa. It stretched, jumped on to the sofa, and walked along it, black and lean. It walked with its tail down. From the sofa it jumped on to a chair, walked across the chairs by the wall, bending down and passing under the arms. It walked to the last of the chairs, jumped on to the floor and sat down in front of the clock, its back to the windows. The pendulum swung back and forth, the old man and the old woman looked sternly at the cat. Then the cat stood up on its hind legs, rested one paw on the clock-case and with the other tried to stop the pendulum. There was no glass in the clock-case. The cat's paw almost touched the pendulum.

Oh, if he could only shout! Nikita, however, cannot move a finger—he cannot budge, it is fearsome, terrible and soon it will be worse....

The moonlight lay immobile in long rectangles on the floor. Everything in the room was silent, sitting back on its haunches. The cat stretched and stretched, bent its head, pressed its ears back and reached the pendulum with its paw. Nikita knew that if the paw touched the pendulum it would stop and at that moment everything would collapse, fall apart with a rattle and clatter and disappear like dust and there would be no drawing-room and no moonlight.

Fear made sharp splinters of glass rattle in Nikita's head and sent shivers over his whole body like sand pouring on it.... Mustering all his strength Nikita threw himself on to the floor with a shriek of despair. And the floor suddenly dropped away beneath him. Nikita sat up. He looked round. In the room there were two frosted windows and through them he could see a strange moon, bigger than usual. On the floor stood a pot and his boots.

"Oh Lord, glory be to God!" said Nikita, hurriedly crossing himself and pushing his head under the pillow. The pillow was soft and warm and packed tight with dreams.

No sooner had he closed his eyes than he could see himself standing on the table in that room again. The pendulum was swinging in the moonlight, the old man and woman were looking down sternly. Again the cat's head appeared from under the sofa. But Nikita had already stretched out his hands, pushed himself off the table and jumped and, his legs moving rapidly, he either flew or floated above the floor. It was exceedingly pleasant to fly about the room. When his feet touched the floor he flapped his arms and slowly rose up to the ceiling and now flew in irregular jerks along the wall. Close to his very nose was the plaster cornice of the room, and on it thick, grey dust that had a cosy smell about it. Then he saw a well-known crack in the wall that looked like the Volga on the map and then an old and very strange nail with a piece of string hanging from it on which dead flies were clustered.

Nikita kicked his foot against the wall and slowly flew across the room to the clock. On the top of the clock-case stood a bronze vase in the bottom of which lay something, he could not make out what. Suddenly a voice seemed to whisper in Nikita's ear, "Take what's there."

Nikita flew to the clock and thrust his hand into the vase. The angry old woman immediately leaned out of her picture on the wall and seized his head in her thin hands. He tore himself away from her but behind him the old man leaned out of the other picture, waved his long pipe and struck Nikita on the back so adroitly that he flew to the floor, gasped and opened his eyes.

The sun sparkled and shone through the frost designs on the windows. Near the bed stood Arkady Ivanovich, shaking Nikita by the shoulder.

"Get up, get up, it's nine o'clock," he said.

When Nikita sat up in bed and rubbed his eyes, Arkady Ivanovich winked several times and rubbed his hands in glee.

"Today, my young friend, there will be no lessons."

"Why?"

"Because why ends in Y. For two weeks you can run around with your tongue hanging out. Get up."

Nikita jumped out of bed and danced on the warm floor.

"Christmas holidays!" He had completely forgotten that today was the beginning of the long and merry fortnight's holiday. As he danced in front of Arkady Ivanovich, Nikita forgot something else—his dream, the vase on the clock and the voice that had whispered in his ear, "Take what's there."

THE OLD HOUSE

Nikita was confronted with fourteen whole days of his own—he could do what he liked. It was even a bit boring.

At breakfast he made a pap of tea, milk, bread and jam and ate so much of it that he had to sit quietly for a time. He gazed at his reflection in the samovar and was surprised that he had such a long, ugly face, a face as long as the samovar was high. Then he thought that if he took a teaspoon and broke it, one piece would make a boat and the other piece would do for a digger, to dig at something or other.

"It's time you went out to play, Nikita," said his mother at last.

Nikita dressed slowly and rubbing his finger along the plastered wall went the whole length of the corridor where the stoves smelt warm and cosy. To the left of this long corridor, on the southern side, were the winter rooms, heated and habitable. To the right, on the northern side, were the five summer rooms, half empty, with the drawing-room in the centre. Here there were huge tiled stoves that were only heated once a week. The crystal chandeliers were wrapped in gauze and on the floor there was a heap of apples—the sweet, slightly putrid smell of them filled the whole of the summer section of the house.

With difficulty Nikita opened the big, oaken double doors and went on tiptoe through the empty rooms. Through the semicircular windows he could see the garden buried under the snow. The trees stood motionless, their white branches bowed, and lilac bushes on either side of the balcony staircase were bent low under the load of snow. The tracks of a hare showed up clearly in the glade. Right beside the window a big-headed crow that looked like a devil sat on a branch.

Nikita tapped at the window and the crow side-stepped and then flew off, brushing the snow from the branch with its wings.

Nikita reached the last corner room. Here dust-covered cupboards stood in a row along the wall and through their glass doors he could see the bindings of old books. Over the tiled fireplace hung the portrait of an extremely beautiful woman. She was dressed in a black velvet riding-habit and her gloved hand held a riding-whip. She seemed to be walking along and to have turned round to look at Nikita with a merry twinkle in her big, penetrating eyes.

Nikita sat down on the sofa and resting his chin in his fists looked at the lady. He could sit for a long time and look at her like that. On account of her—he had heard it several times from his mother—his great-grandfather had suffered some terrible misfortunes. The portrait of the unfortunate great-grandfather hung over

21

the bookcase—he was a skinny old man with a sharp nose and deep sunken eyes; he held a beringed hand pressed to the breast of a dressing-gown; by his side lay a half-unrolled papyrus and a quill-pen. Everything pointed to the fact that he was a very unhappy old man.

Mamma had told him that his great-grandfather used to sleep during the day and at night he used to read and write; he went out to walk only at dusk. At night watchmen walked round the house sounding their rattles so that the night-birds would not fly under the windows and scare great-grandfather. It is said that in those days the garden was overgrown with thick, tall grass. All the house, except these rooms, was locked up and was not inhabited. The household servants had run away. Great-grandfather's affairs were in a piteous state.

One day he was not to be found in his study, in the house or in the garden—they searched for him a whole week but could not find him. Five years later his heir received a strange letter which he sent from Siberia: "I sought tranquillity in wisdom and found oblivion in nature."

The cause of all these strange happenings was the lady in the riding-habit. Nikita looked at her curiously and excitely.

The crow again appeared outside the window, disturbed the snow as it alighted on the branch, dipped its head, opened its bill and cawed. This gave Nikita a feeling of awe. He left the empty rooms and ran out into the yard.

AT THE WELL

At the well in the middle of the yard, where the snow was yellow, trampled and frozen hard, Nikita found Mishka Koryashonok. Mishka sat on the edge of the well and was dipping the end of a leather mitten which he wore on his hand in the water.

Nikita asked him why he was doing it.

22

"All the Konchan boys dip mittens in water and we're going to do it too," answered Mishka Koryashonok. "They get hard and are awfully good to fight with. Are you going to the village?"

"When?"

"We'll have dinner and then go. But don't tell your mother."

"Mamma let me go out but told me not to fight."

"What d'you mean, not to fight? And if someone goes for you? I'll tell you who'll go for you—Styopka Karnaushkin. He'll give you what for and down you go."

"Ugh, I can manage Styopka," said Nikita, "I can fix him with my little finger." He showed Mishka his finger.

Koryashonok looked at it, spat and said in a rough voice:

"Styopka Karnaushkin's fist has been bewitched. Last week he went to Utyovka with his father for salt and fish, and there he had his fist bewitched—may my eyes burst if I tell a lie."

Nikita pondered over that—of course it would be better not to go to the village at all but then Mishka would call him a coward.

"And how was his fist bewitched?" he asked.

Mishka spat again.

"Easy as anything. First you take soot and rub it on your hand, then you say three times, 'Tannybanny, what's under us, under the iron posts?' And that's all...."

Nikita looked admiringly at Koryashonok. Just then the yard gates opened with a creak and sheep ran out in a solid grey mass—their hoofs rattling like castanets, their tails wagging and droppings falling. The flock of sheep swarmed around the well. Bleating and pushing each other the sheep scrambled up to the well, broke the thin ice with their muzzles, drank and coughed. A dirty, long-wooled ram stared at Mishka with his white-spotted eyes and stamped his feet. Mishka said to him, "Lazy-bones," and the ram ran at him and Mishka just managed to jump across the well. Nikita and Mishka ran across the yard jeering at the ram. The ram started after them, thought better of it and bleated as though it were saying, "Lazy-bones yourselves."

When Nikita was called from the back porch to come in to lunch Mishka Koryashonok said:

"See you don't let us down—we're going to the village!"

THE BATTLE

Nikita and Mishka Koryashonok took the short road to the village across the garden and the pond. Where the wind had blown the snow off the ice Mishka stopped for a minute, took out his penknife and a box of matches, sat down, sniffed around for a bit and then began to dig into the blue ice where there was a white bubble in it. These bubbles were called "cats"—they were formed by swamp gases that rose from the bottom of the pond and froze into the ice as bubbles. Mishka cut through the ice till he reached the bubble, then struck a match and held it to the gas-well; a yellowish flame that burnt silently rose over the ice.

"Don't tell anybody about it," said Mishka, "and next week we'll go down to the lower pond and set light to the 'cats,' there's one there I know—as big as a house—it'll burn a whole day."

The boys ran across the pond, scrambled through the flattened yellow reeds on the far bank and reached the village.

There had been a lot of snow that winter. Where the wind blew freely between the houses there was little snow, but at the sides of the houses, where there was no wind, it had piled up to the roofs.

The hut of the crazy, landless peasant Savoska was completely buried, only the chimney sticking out of the snow. Mishka said that three days before the whole village had turned out to dig Savoska out of the snow but he, the fool, when he was snowed under at night had lit the stove, made himself some vegetable soup without meat, had eaten it and then climbed up on the stove to sleep. They found him asleep on the stove, had awakened him and pulled his ears for his foolishness.

The village was empty and quiet, smoke curled lazily from some of the chimneys. A hazy sun hung low over the white plain and over the snow-covered haystacks and roofs. Nikita and Mishka went to the cottage of Artamon Tyurin, a formidable-looking peasant that everybody in the village feared, so strong and ill-tempered was he; Nikita peeped in at the little window and saw Artamon's stiff beard—like a red bass broom—he was sitting at the table eating something out of a wooden bowl. At the other window three freckled boys, Artamon's sons, Syomka, Lyonka and Artamoshka Junior, stood with their noses pressed against the glass.

When Mishka approached the cottage he whistled and Artamon turned round, his big jaws busily chewing, and threatened him with a spoon. The three boys disappeared from the window and immediately appeared on the porch, tying their sheepskin coats on with girdles.

"Ugh, you," said Mishka, pushing his cap over one ear, "ugh, you, girls. . . . Sitting at home . . . scared. . . ."

"We ain't scared of anything," answered one of the freckle-faces—Syomka.

"Papa says we mustn't wear our felt boots out," said Lyonka.

"I went out before and shouted at the Konchan gang but they didn't take any notice," said Artamoshka Junior.

Mishka pushed his cap on to the other ear, clicked his tongue and spoke in tones of decision:

"Come on, we'll razz 'em. We'll show 'em."

The freckle-faces answered, "All right," and all together they climbed up a huge snowdrift that lay across the street—from here, beyond Artamon's cottage, the "other end" of the village began.

Nikita thought that there must be crowds of boys on the Konchan side of the drift but there were only two little girls, wrapped in shawls, who pulled a sled up the drift, got on to it and, sticking their felt-booted feet out in front, seized the rope and with squeaks raced across the street past the barn and then down the steep bank on to the ice of the river.

Mishka, and with him the freckle-faces and Nikita, began shouting from their position on the snowdrift.

"Hi, Konchan!"

"We're after you!"

"You're all scared and hiding!"

"Come on out, we'll bash you!"

"Come out, we'll fight you one-handed, hi, Konchan!" shouted Mishka, slapping his leather mittens.

Four Konchan boys appeared on the other side of the drift. Slapping their mittens and smoothing them by rubbing them up and down on their sides, they straightened their caps and also began to shout:

"Fat lot we care for you!"

"Think you can scare us!"

"Froggie, froggie, kva, kva, kva!"

26

The gang came up from Nikita's side of the drift—Alyosha, Nil and Vanka Black Ears, Savoska's nephew Petrushka and another tiny little boy with a big stomach, his mother's shawl on his head with the ends crossed on his chest. On the Konchan side there were also another five or six boys.

"Hi, you, freckle-mugs," they shouted, "we'll rub your freckles off."

"Cock-eyed blacksmiths, shod a mouse!" shouted Mishka Korya-shonok from his side.

"Froggie, froggie!"

About forty boys had gathered on the two sides. But nobody seemed anxious to start—they were all scared. They threw snowballs, thumbed their noses. From the far side they shouted, "Froggie, froggie!" from Nikita's side, "Cock-eyed blacksmiths!" Both these were insults. Suddenly a smallish, broad-shouldered, pug-nosed lad appeared amongst the Konchan gang.

"Hi, frogs, come on, one against one!"

This was the famous Styopka Karnaushkin with the bewitched fist.

The Kanchan boys threw up their caps and whistled shrilly. On Nikita's side the boys remained silent. Nikita took a good look. The freckled boys stood still and scowled. Alyosha and Vanka Black Ears—moved back, the little boy in his mother's shawl rolled his big round eyes at Karnaushkin and looked ready to cry, Mishka Koryashonok, pulling his homespun girdle down under his stomach, muttered:

"I had 'em tougher than this. It won't be the first time. I don't like beginning but when I get my rag out, I'll give it him, knock his hat ten yards off his block."

Styopka Karnaushkin, seeing that nobody was anxious to fight him, beckoned with his mitten to his side.

"At 'em, boys!"

27

And the Konchan gang with shouts and whistles came racing down the snowdrift.

The freckle-faces got scared and fled, after them ran Mishka, Vanka Black Ears and then all the other boys: Nikita fled as well. The small boy in the shawl sat down in the snow and cried.

Our side ran through Artamon's yard and Chernoukhov's and gathered on another drift. Nikita looked back. On the snow lay Alyosha, Nil and five of our side—some had fallen, some lay down out of sheer fright—you couldn't hit a man lying down.

Nikita stood up; he could have cried for shame: they were all cowards and had been afraid to fight. He stood still, his fists clenched and saw that Styopka Karnaushkin, pug-nosed and big-mouthed, with a lock of hair hanging down from under his sheepskin cap, was rushing towards him.

Nikita lowered his head and marching towards him hit Styopka in the chest with all his might. Styopka shook his head, dropped his cap and sat down in the snow.

"O-oh, you, that's enough," he said.

The Konchan boys immediately stopped. Nikita went towards them and they gave way. Out-running Nikita and shouting, "We're winning," the boys fell on the Konchan gang like a solid wall. The Konchan gang fled. They chased them through five or six yards until they all lay down.

Nikita went back to his own end of the village, excited, overheated, looking for somebody else to fight.

Somebody called him. Behind a barn stood Styopka Karnaushkin. Nikita went up to him and Styopka frowned at him.

"You gave me a good 'un," he said. "Want to make friends?"

"Of course I do," Nikita answered hurriedly.

The boys smiled, looking at each other.

"Let's swop," said Styopka.

"Let's."

Nikita wondered for a minute what was the best thing he could give Styopka, and then gave him his penknife with four blades. Styopka put his hand into his pocket and pulled out a knuckle-bone cast from lead.

"Here you are, don't lose it, it's worth a lot."

HOW A DULL EVENING ENDED

That evening Nikita sat looking at the pictures in the *Niva* magazine and reading the legends under them. There was very little of interest.

One picture showed a woman standing on a door-step with arms bare to the elbow: she had flowers in her hair; on her shoulders and at her feet were pigeons. A man with a gun over his shoulder was grinning at her from beyond a fence.

The most annoying thing about the picture was that he could not tell why it had been drawn. The explanation said:

"Who of you has not seen tame pigeons, those real friends of man?" (Nikita skipped the rest about the pigeons.) "Who has not enjoyed throwing grain to these birds in the morning? The talented German artist, Hans Wurst, has recorded such a moment. Young Elsa, the daughter of a pastor, has come out of the house. The pigeons see their beloved mistress and joyfully fly to her feet. See how one of them is sitting on her shoulder while another eats from her hand. A young neighbour, a sportsman, is secretly admiring the picture."

Nikita would imagine that Elsa had nothing else to do but to feed pigeons—what boredom. Her father, the pastor, would be somewhere in a room, sitting on a chair and yawning from boredom. And the young neighbour is grimacing as though he had a stomach-ache, and he would go down the road, grinning like that, and his gun would not shoot, of course. The sky in the picture was grey and the sunlight was grey.

Nikita sucked the point of his pencil and drew moustaches on the pastor's daughter.

The next picture was a view of the town of Buzuluk: a milestone and a broken wheel by the roadside, and in the distance, board huts, a little church and rain slanting down from heavy clouds.

Nikita yawned and closed *Niva*, leaned on the table and listened.

From the attic above came whistling sounds and a long drawn-out blowing. Then came the heavy bass "Oo-oo-oo-oo-oo," drawling, frowning and puffing. Then with a trill the sound changed to a thin, plaintive tone and whistled down one nostril in a tormented voice as thin as a cotton thread. Again the bass came into play together with the puffing.

Over the round table hung a lamp under a white porcelain shade. Somebody walked heavily along the passage on the other side of the wall—apparently the furnaceman—and the crystal ornaments under the lamp rattled.

Mamma's head was bent over a book, her hair was ash-blonde, soft and fine, and curled on her temple where there was a birth-mark like a millet seed. From time to time Mamma would cut the pages with a knitting-needle. Her book had a brick-coloured cover. The bookcase in Papa's study was full of such books and they were all called *European News*. He wondered how adults could like such boring books: reading a book like that was as bad as rubbing a brick.

On Mamma's lap slept Akhilka, the tame hedgehog, his wet pig's nose resting on his paws. When people went to bed at night he would already have slept his fill and would wander all night about the house, stamping with his claws, grunting and smelling in all the corners, looking into the mouse-holes.

On the other side of the wall the furnaceman made a clatter with an iron door and they could hear how he stirred up the fire. The room smelt of warm plaster and washed floors. It was boring but cosy. Up there in the attic there was a great effort at whistling—"yuee-yuee-yuee."

"Mamma, who's that whistling?"

Mamma raised her brows but did not look up from her book. Arkady Ivanovich, who was drawing lines in his notebook, seemed only to have been waiting for that question.

"When we speak of an inanimate object," he said with the rapidity of one who has learned something by heart, "we employ the pronoun 'what.'"

"Booo-oo-oo-oo," came the howl from the attic. Mamma raised her head, listened, eased her shoulders and drew her woollen shawl closer about them. The hedgehog woke up and snorted angrily.

Nikita could picture the snow blowing in through the little glassless window of the cold, dark attic. Between the huge ceiling beams, where the doves used to perch, lay with the springs sticking out old broken chairs, armchairs and pieces of old sofas. On one of these armchairs, close against the chimney sat "Wind," hairy, covered in dust and cobwebs. He sat still, his cheeks resting in his hands, and howled, "Bo-o-o-o-ring." The night was long, the attic cold and he sat there, lonely old soul, and howled. Nikita slid off his chair and sat down near his mother. She smiled lovingly at him, pulled Nikita towards her and kissed him on the forehead.

"Isn't it time for you to go to bed?"

"Oh, please, another half hour."

Nikita leaned his head on his mother's shoulder. In the depth of the room a door creaked and the cat Vaska appeared—his tail held high, his whole appearance expressing humility and good-will. He opened his pink mouth and mewed so softly it could scarcely be heard. Without raising his eyes from the exercise-book Arkady Ivanovich asked:

"On what business have you come, Vasily Vasilievich?"

Vaska walked over to Mamma, looked at her with his green eyes narrowed to tiny slits and mewed in louder tones. The hedgehog again grunted. Nikita thought that Vaska knew something, that he had come to tell them something.

The wind howled desperately in the attic. Just then there came a subdued shout from outside the windows, there was a crunching of snow and the sound of voices. Mamma got up quickly. Akhilka grunted and rolled off her lap.

Arkady Ivanovich ran to the window and looked out.

"They've come!" he exclaimed.

32

"Good God!" said Mamma excitedly. "Surely that can't be Anna Apollosovna? In this blizzard. . . ."

A few minutes later, Nikita, who stood in the passage, saw the heavy, felt-covered door open; a cloud of frosty steam rushed in followed by a tall, stout woman in two fur coats and a shawl all covered with snow. She held by the hand a boy in a grey coat with shining buttons and a Cossack hood. Behind them, stamping in the frozen felt boots, came the coachman with an icy beard, yellow icicles in place of a moustache and white fluffy eyebrows. In his arms he carried a little girl in a white goatskin coat with the fur outside. She lay with her eyes closed, her head resting on the coachman's shoulder; her face was sweet and roguish.

As she came in, the tall woman exclaimed in a loud bass:

"Alexandra Leontievna, your guests have come!" and lifting her hands she began to unwind her shawl. "Don't come near us, we'll give you a cold. I must say your roads are just rotten. . . . Right close to the house we ran into some bushes."

This was Mamma's friend Anna Apollosovna Babkina who lived in Samara. Her son Victor, waiting for somebody to take his hood off, looked frowningly at Nikita. Mamma took the sleeping girl from the coachman, removed her fur hood—a wealth of bright golden locks immediately burst out from it—and kissed her.

"Lilechka, you've arrived."

The girl sighed, opened her big blue eyes and sighed a second time as she woke up.

VICTOR AND LILYA

Nikita and Victor Babkin awoke early next morning in Nikita's room; sitting up in their beds they looked at each other with knitted brows:

"I remember you," said Nikita.

"I remember you very well," answered Victor immediately. "You came to see us in Samara once and you ate so much duck and apple sauce that they gave you castor oil."

"That I don't remember."

"But I do."

The boys sat in silence. Victor deliberately yawned.

"I have a tutor—Arkady Ivanovich," said Nikita carelessly. "He's awful strict, stuffs me full of knowledge. He can read any book in half an hour."

Victor sneered.

"I'm going to the Gymnasium, the second class. They're so strict there that they keep me without lunch all the time."

"So what of it!" said Nikita.

"It's something. Although I can go a thousand days without eating if I want to."

"Huh," said Nikita, "have you tried?"

"I haven't tried it yet, Mamma won't let me."

Nikita yawned and stretched.

34

"Day before yesterday I beat Styopka Karnaushkin."

"And who's Styopka Karnaushkin?"

"Strongest kid in the village. I got him such a one—boom, and down he went. I gave him my penknife with four blades and he gave me a lead knuckle-bone. I'll show you later on."

Nikita slipped out of bed and slowly began to dress himself.

"And I can lift the Makarov Dictionary with one hand," muttered Victor in a voice that trembled from vexation, but it was clear that he was already giving up.

Nikita went over to the tiled stove with the sleeping-shelf, jumped up on to it without touching it with his hands, lifted up one foot and jumped down to the floor on the other foot.

"If you move your legs fast enough you can fly," he said, looking attentively at Victor.

"That's nothing. A lot of boys in our class can fly."

The boys dressed and went down to the dining-room where there was a smell of hot bread and buns, where so much steam came from the brightly polished samovar and curled up to the ceiling that the windows were all steamed up. Mamma, Arkady Ivanovich and the girl of yesterday, Lilya—a youngster of about nine and Victor's sister—were already seated at table. From the neighbouring room came the sound of Anna Apollosovna's deep bass: "Please give me a towel."

Lilya was dressed in a white frock with a light

blue sash that was tied behind her in a bow. In her curly fair hair there was another bow tied butterfly-fashion, also light blue.

Nikita went up to her, flushed and bowed. Lilya turned round on her chair, held out her hand and said very seriously:

"Good-morning, boy."

As she said those words she raised her upper lip.

It seemed to Nikita that this was not a real girl, she was so pretty, especially her eyes—they were blue and brighter than the ribbons—and her long silky lashes. Lilya, paying no further attention to Nikita, took up a big teacup with both hands and buried her face in it. The boys sat down together. Victor, it seemed, drank tea like a baby—he bent over the cup and sucked tea out of it with his long lips. He secretly piled sugar into his cup until the tea became thick and then asked in a weak voice for water to be added.

"D'you like my sister?' he whispered, nudging Nikita with his knee.

Nikita did not answer but only blushed.

"You be careful with her," whispered Victor, "the kid always goes complaining to Mamma."

In the meantime Lilya had finished her tea, wiped her mouth on a napkin and got down slowly from her chair. She went up to Alexandra Leontievna.

"Thank you, Auntie Sasha," she said politely and punctiliously.

Then she went over to the window, sat down with her feet drawn up under her in a huge brown armchair, got a box of needles and thread from somewhere and settled down to sew. All that Nikita could now see was the huge butterfly bow, two hanging curls and between them the moving tip of a tongue that was stuck out ever so slightly and with which Lilya helped herself along with her sewing.

All Nikita's thoughts were hopelessly mixed up. He began to show Victor how to jump over the back of a chair, but Lilya did not turn her head and Mamma said:

36

"Children, if you want to make a noise go out into the yard."

The boys got dressed and went out. It was a misty, warm day. The reddish sun hung low over long layers of cloud banks that looked like snow-covered fields. Rosy trees, covered in hoar-frost, stood in the garden. The indistinct shadows on the snow reflected that same warm light. It was unusually calm, the only sound coming from two dogs, Sharok and Katok, who stood side by side near the back porch, their heads turned towards each other, growling. They could stand there growling, baring their teeth and stamping around for a long time, until one of the workers came along and threw a mitten at them, when they would cough with anger, rise up on their hind legs and fight so that the fur flew. They were afraid of other dogs, hated beggars and at nights, instead of guarding the house, slept in the coach-house.

"What are you going to do?" asked Victor.

Nikita looked at a ragged discontented crow that flew from the barn to the cowshed. He did not want to play, and for a reason that he did not understand, he was sad. He would have suggested going into the drawing-room, where there was a sofa, and reading something but Victor said:

"Huh, I see you can only play with girls."

"Why?" asked Nikita, flushing.

"Because—you know yourself why."

"You leave me alone. I don't know what you're talking about. Let's go to the well."

The boys went to the well towards which the cows were coming through the open gates to drink. In the distance Mishka Koryashonok was cracking a huge herdsman's whip with a sound like a gun.

"Bayan, Bayan," he shouted suddenly. "Look out, Nikita!"

Nikita looked behind him. Bayan, a rosy-grey, short-horn bull with curly locks on its forehead, was moving towards the boys.

"Moo-oo-o," roared Bayan intermittently, swishing his sides with his tail.

"Run, Victor!" shouted Nikita and seizing him by the sleeve ran towards the house.

The bull went after the boys at a trot. "Moo-oo-oo."

Victor looked behind him, shrieked, fell in the snow and covered his head with his arms. Bayan was no more than five paces from him. Nikita stopped, suddenly grew hot with anger, tore off his cap, ran to the bull and began beating it in the face.

"Get away, get away!"

The bull stood still and lowered its horns. Mishka Koryashonok ran up from the other side cracking his whip. Bayan mooed plaintively, turned round and went back to the well. Nikita's lips were trembling from the excitement. He put on his cap and turned round. Victor was already near the house and from there beckoned to him with his hand. Nikita happened to look up at the window—the third to the left from the porch. In the window he saw two astonished blue eyes and over them a big butterfly bow that stood up straight. Lilya, who had climbed on to the window-sill, was looking at Nikita and suddenly smiled. Nikita immediately turned away. He did not look at the window again. He was happy now and he shouted:

"Victor, let's go sliding down the hills, hurry up!"

Right up to lunch-time they slid down the hills, laughing and "going mad." All the time Nikita kept secretly wondering:

"When I go home and pass the window shall I look up at it or shall I look the other way? No, I won't look at it."

At lunch Nikita tried not to look at Lilya and even if he had tried to look at her he would not have succeeded because between him and the girl sat Anna Apollosovna in a red velvet jacket; waving her arms she spoke in such a loud and deep bass voice that the glass ornaments under the lamp all tinkled.

"No, no, Alexandra Leontievna," she boomed, "teach your son at home. In the Gymnasium there is such disgusting mismanagement, I could take that director with my own hands and throw him out.... Victor!" she exclaimed suddenly, "you're not to listen to what your mother says about grown-ups, you must respect your superiors. And take our teachers, Alexandra Leontievna, the crassest idiots. Each of them sillier than the other. And their geography teacher? What's his name, Victor?"

"Sinichkin."

"I've told you it's not Sinichkin but Sinyavkin. That teacher is such a fool that one day in the hall, after he'd been to visit us, instead of putting on his cap he picked up a cat that had been sleeping on the trunk and put it on his head.... Victor, how are you holding that knife and fork? Don't champ.... And move your chair closer to the table.... What was it I wanted to tell you, Alexandra Leontievna? Oh, yes, I've brought a whole bag full of odds and ends for the Christmas tree.... Tomorrow we'll have to get the children busy pasting them up."

"I think they ought to start today," said Mamma, "otherwise they won't be ready in time."

"Do as you think best. I'm going to write some letters. Thank you, my friend, for the lunch."

Anna Apollosovna wiped her lips with a napkin, moved her chair back with a great deal of noise and went into her bedroom with the

intention of writing letters, but a minute later the bedsprings creaked as violently as if an elephant had flopped on them.

After the cloth had been cleared off the big table Mamma brought four pairs of scissors and began to make paste. She did it this way: from the cupboard in the corner, where the family medicines were kept, Mamma got a jar of starch, shook about a spoonful into a glass, put in a couple of teaspoons of cold water and mixed it all into a paste. Then she poured in boiling water from the samovar and stirred it until it was clear like a jelly. This made an excellent paste.

The boys brought in Anna Apollosovna's leather bag and put it on the table. Mamma opened it and began to take out the contents: sheets of gold paper, smooth and stamped, sheets of silver, blue, green and orange paper, Bristol-board, boxes of candles and Christmas-tree candlesticks, boxes of goldfish and coloured cockerels, boxes of hollow glass balls threaded on strings, others with glass balls that had silver hooks on top and depressions painted in different colours on four sides,

40

still more boxes full of crackers, bunches of gold and silver tinsel, lanterns with coloured mica windows and a big star. With each new discovery the children groaned with delight.

"There are some more good things," said Mamma, dipping her hands into the bag, "but for the time being we shall not unwrap them all. Let's get on with the gluing."

Victor began to make chains, Nikita made paper cones for sweets while Mamma cut paper and cardboard.

"Auntie Sasha, may I make a little box?" asked Lilya very politely.

"Make whatever you like, my dear."

The children began to work in silence, breathing heavily through their noses and wiping their starchy hands on their clothes. While they were working Mamma told them that in the old days there were no decorations for Christmas trees to be had and everything had to be made by hand. Some people were so clever at it, she had seen it herself, that they could make a whole castle with towers and winding staircases and drawbridges. In front of the castle there was a lake made of mirror surrounded by moss. On the pond there was a golden bark drawn by two swans.

Lilya listened, working in silence, occasionally helping herself with the tip of her tongue. Nikita left his paper cones and looked at her. Mamma went out of the room at that moment. Victor hung about ten yards of different coloured paper chains on the chairs.

"What are you making?" asked Nikita.

Without lifting her head Lilya smiled and cut a star out of gold paper and pasted it on the blue lid of the box.

"What do you want that box for?" asked Nikita softly.

"The box is for dolls' gloves," answered Lilya seriously. "You're a boy and you don't understand such things." She raised her head and looked at Nikita with severe blue eyes.

41

He began to blush, got redder and hotter until he was crimson all over.

"How red you are," said Lilya, "like a beetroot."

Again she bent over her box. Her face had a roguish smile on it. Nikita sat as though he were glued to the chair. He did not know what to say next and he could not have left the room however hard he tried. The girl laughed at him, but he did not take offence, was not angry but only stared at her. Suddenly Lilya spoke to him again, this time in a different voice and without raising her eyes, as though there were already some secret between them.

"D'you like the box?" she said.

"Yes. I like it," answered Nikita.

"I like it, too, I like it very much," she said rocking her head back and forth which made her bow and her curls sway. She wanted to add something but Victor came along and thrust his head between Nikita and Lilya.

"What box, where's the box?" he asked. "Huh, rubbishy little box, I can make as many as you want of them...."

"Victor, honestly I'll tell Mamma that you don't let me get on with my work," she said in a trembling voice. She took her glue and paper and went to the other end of the table.

Victor winked at Nikita.

"I told you you'd have to be careful with her—she tells everything to Mother."

Late that evening, as they lay in bed in the dark room, Nikita, the bedclothes over his head, spoke in a dull voice from under the blankets.

"Victor, are you asleep?"

"Not yet.... I don't know.... What?"

"Listen, Victor.... I've got to tell you a terrible secret. Victor.... Don't sleep.... Victor, listen...."

"Hm-m-m, Phew-ew-ew-ew-ew," answered Victor.

42

THE PRESENT ON A SEPARATE SLEIGH

It was only just daybreak when Nikita heard somebody raking in the stoves; then a door banged at the end of the passage—that was the furnaceman bringing in bundles of firewood and dung briquettes.

Nikita awoke in a joyful mood. The morning was bright and frosty.

The window was covered in a thick layer of floral designs in frost. Victor was still asleep, Nikita threw a pillow at him, but he merely grunted and pulled the blankets over his head. Out of sheer joy Nikita slipped quickly out of bed, dressed and then began wondering where to go; he ran first to Arkady Ivanovich.

Arkady Ivanovich had only just awakened and was reading the same letter that he had already read some thirty times. When he saw Nikita he raised his feet with the blankets over them and brought them down with a crash on the bed.

"How extraordinary!" he shouted. "You're the first one up!"

"Arkady Ivanovich, it's a wonderful day today."

"Yes, my boy, it is a wonderful day."

"Arkady Ivanovich, there's something I want to ask you." Nikita ran his finger along the lintel of the door. "Do you like the Babkins very much?"

"Which of the Babkins do you mean?"

"The children."

"So? And which of the children do you want me to like?"

Although Arkady Ivanovich spoke in a very ordinary voice he said it very quickly. He leaned his elbows on the pillow and looked at Nikita without a smile, it is true, but very attentively. Apparently he also knew something. Nikita suddenly turned round and ran out of the room, thought a bit and then went out into the yard.

Over the workers' quarters, over the bathhouse in the gully and farther on, beyond the white fields, over the whole village rose columns of blue smoke. During the night the hoar-frost on the trees had become still thicker and the branches of the huge black poplars over the pond were hanging down quite low from the weight of the snow; they made a clear silhouette against the blue frosty sky. The snow scintillated and crackled. The frost made his nose sting and clung to his eyelashes.

On a heap of still faintly smoking ashes near the back porch Sharok and Katok were growling at each other. Mishka Koryashonok, with a thick stick in his hand, came floundering through the snow straight towards Nikita; he was going to play a sort of hockey game with frozen snowballs. Just at that moment a string of horse-drawn sleighs appeared to the right of the village. One by one they crawled out of the gully and swayed along, low and black against the snow, past the lower pond to the dam.

Mishka Koryashonok, placing the thumb of his mitten against a nostril, blew his nose.

"They're our sleighs returning from the city with the presents," he said.

The sleighs were now crossing the dam under the arch formed by the snow-covered willows and the boys could hear the crunching of the snow, the whistle of the sleigh runners and the heavy breathing of the horses.

The first to enter the yard, leading the procession of sleighs as usual, was the old worker Nikifor on a big roan mare Vesta. Nikifor, a sturdily built old man, walked easily beside the string of sleighs in frozen felt boots bound round with rope. His long, heavy sheepskin coat was thrown open, the upturned fur collar, his cap and his beard were all white with frost. His mare Vesta, her sides pumping and sweating all over, stood in a cloud of steam. As he walked along

44

Nikifor shouted to the last sleighs in a strong voice that was hoarse from a cold:

"Hi, turn towards the barns—and the last sleigh is to go to the house!"

The train consisted of sixteen sleighs. The horses pulled up smartly, there was a strong smell of horse sweat, whips cracked, sleigh runners wheezed and a cloud of steam stood over the procession.

When the last sleigh had left the dam and drew nearer Nikita could not at first make out what was on it. It was big, strange in form, green and with a red stripe. Nikita's heart began to beat faster. On the sleigh, behind which a second pair of runners had been attached, a sharp-bowed, two-oared boat creaked and swayed. Lying alongside the boat were two green oars and a mast with a copper ball on top.

So this was the present that he had been promised in the mysterious letter.

THE CHRISTMAS TREE

A big frozen fir-tree was dragged into the drawing-room. Pakhom spent a long time chipping and hammering with his axe to fix it into the wooden cross that it was to stand on. At last they lifted up the tree and it was so high that the delicate green top was bent over under the ceiling.

There was a waft of cold from the tree, but gradually the frozen branches thawed and spread out to their normal positions; the odour of fir needles filled the house. The children brought a heap of paper chains and boxes of decorations into the drawing-room, placed chairs around the tree and began trimming it. They found they had not made enough. They had to paste together more cones for the sweets, paint walnuts with gold paint and tie silver threads to the little spice-cakes and big Crimean apples. The children spent the whole evening at this work until Lilya, resting her head with its crumpled bow on her arms, dropped off to sleep.

Christmas Eve came. The decoration of the tree was completed, they covered it with gold tinsel, hung up chains and fixed the candles in their little coloured holders. When everything was ready Mamma said:

"And now go away until evening, children; don't you dare even glance into the drawing-room."

That day they lunched late and in a great hurry—the children had nothing but an apple charlotte. The house was in an uproar. The boys wandered about the house, worrying everybody, asking how much longer they had to wait till evening. Even Arkady Ivanovich—he had changed into a tail-coat and a starched shirt that stood out like a box—did not know what to do with himself and wandered from window to window whistling. Lilya went to her mother.

The sun crawled towards the earth's rim with terrible slowness, it turned a rosy hue, hazy clouds spread over it, the purple shadows thrown by the well on the white snow grew longer. At last Mamma told the boys to go and get dressed. On his bed Nikita found a blue silk Russian blouse with herring-bone embroidery on the collar, cuffs and skirt, a corded silk girdle with tassels and baggy, velvet knickerbockers. He dressed and ran to his mother, who parted his hair with a comb, took him by the shoulders, looked him straight in the face and then took him over to a big pier-glass framed in mahogany.

In the mirror Nikita saw a nicely-dressed, well-mannered boy. Surely that could not be he?

"Oh, Nikita, Nikita," sighed his mother as she kissed his head, "if you were always such a nice boy!"

Nikita tiptoed out of the room and saw a girl in white walking importantly down the passage towards him. She was wearing a gorgeous white dress with muslin petticoats, a big white bow in her hair and six fat curls on either side of her face—also unrecognizable—falling on to her thin shoulders. Lilya walked up to Nikita and looked at him with a grimace.

"Did you think I was a ghost?" she asked. "What are you scared of?" and she walked into the study and sat down on the sofa with her legs drawn up under her.

Nikita followed her into the room and also sat down on the sofa but at the other end. The stove had been lit, the logs crackled and shed live coals. A flickering, reddish light lit up the backs of the leather chairs, the corner of the gilded frame on the wall and the bust of Pushkin that stood between the two bookcases.

Lilya sat motionless. It was wonderful, the way the light from the stove lit up her cheek and her retroussé nose. Victor appeared wearing a blue uniform with shining buttons and a collar of gold braid so tight that it was difficult for him to talk.

Victor sat down in an armchair, also without speaking. In the drawing-room near by they could hear Mamma and Anna Apollosovna—they were undoing packages, they stood something on the floor and were talking in low voices. Victor would have liked to look through the keyhole but it was pasted over with paper on the other side.

Then the outside door was slammed, they heard a number of voices and the steps of many tiny feet. The children from the village had arrived. He should have run to greet them but Nikita could not move. A warm bluish light glowed through the frost-patterns on the windows. Then Lilya spoke in a thin, small voice:

"A star has come out."

Just then the study doors were thrown open. The children jumped off the sofa. In the drawing-room, from floor to ceiling, the Christmas tree gleamed with many, many candles. It was like a fire-tree flashing gold, sparks and long rays of light. It was a heavy light that smelled of warmth, fir needles, wax, tangerines and spice-cakes.

The children stood motionless, astounded. The outer doors to the drawing-room were also opened and the village children came in and pressed close against each other and to the wall. They had all removed their felt boots and wore thick woollen stockings—they were dressed in red, pink and yellow shirts, yellow, crimson and white kerchiefs.

Mamma began to play a polka on the piano. As she played she turned towards the tree with a smile on her face and sang:

> *The heron he has legs so long,*
> *But couldn't find the way back home. . . .*

Nikita held out his hand to Lilya. She gave him her hand but continued to look at the tree which was reflected in detail in her blue eyes, one tree in each eye. The children stood quite still.

Arkady Ivanovich ran over to the crowd of boys and girls, took them by the hands and began to gallop round the tree with them. The tails of his coat flew out. As he ran round he grabbed two more children, then Nikita and Lilya and Victor and at last all the children had joined hands and were dancing round the Christmas tree.

> *Now I'm hiding gold, hiding gold,*
> *Now I'm hiding silver, silver,*

sang the village children.

Nikita pulled a cracker from the Christmas tree and broke it; inside there was a tall pointed cap with a star on it. Soon crackers were popping everywhere, there was a smell of gunpowder and a rustling of tissue-paper caps.

Lilya got a paper pinafore with pockets. She put it on. Her cheeks were red like apples, her lips were smeared with chocolate. She was laughing all the time as she looked at a huge doll seated beneath the Christmas tree on a big basket with a complete doll's layette.

Under the tree there were also paper packets for the village boys and girls wrapped in varicoloured kerchiefs. Victor got a whole regiment of soldiers with cannon and tents and Nikita a real leather saddle and bridle with a riding-whip.

Now came the sound of cracking nuts, shells crunched underfoot and the children breathed heavily through their noses as they unwrapped their presents.

Mamma again played the piano, the children danced and sang round the Christmas tree, but the candles were already burning low

and Arkady Ivanovich, jumping up and down, put them out. The tree grew duller. Mamma closed the piano and told them all to go into the dining-room for tea.

Arkady Ivanovich, however, did not stop—he formed the children in a long chain, he at the head and twenty-five boys and girls behind him, and ran out through the passage and by the longest route into the dining-room.

In the hall Lilya broke away from the chain and stood still to catch her breath, looking at Nikita with laughing eyes. They were close to the hallstand where the heavy coats were hanging.

"What are you laughing at?" asked Lilya.

"You're laughing yourself," answered Nikita.

"And what are you looking at me for?"

Nikita blushed, drew nearer to her and, not knowing himself how it happened, bent down towards Lilya and kissed her. She immediately responded with a rapid speech:

"You're a nice boy, I haven't told you because I didn't want anybody to know, it's a secret." She turned round and ran into the dining-room.

After tea Arkady Ivanovich arranged a game of forfeits but the children were tired, had eaten too much and had no clear idea of what they were supposed to do. At last one tiny boy in a spotted shirt dozed right off, fell from his chair and began to cry loudly.

Mamma said that the Christmas-tree party was over. The children went out into the passage where their felt boots and sheepskin coats lay along the wall. They dressed and poured out into the frosty night in a bunch.

Nikita went with the children as far as the dam. As he made his way back home, the moon shone in a pale, multicoloured ring high up in the heavens. The trees on the dam and in the garden were huge and white and they seemed to have grown taller in the moonlight. To-his right a white frosty desert stretched far away into impenetrable darkness. A shadow with a big head and long legs moved by Nikita's side.

Nikita felt as if he were walking in his sleep through some enchanted kingdom. Only in a kingdom of magic could it be so strange and at the same time so joyous.

VICTOR'S MISFORTUNE

During the holidays Victor made friends with Mishka Koryashonok and went to the lower pond with him to set fire to the "cats." One they fired was so big that the flames leaped out of the ice to more than the height of a man. Then they built a fortress in the ditch beyond the pond—a turret of snow with a wall round it complete with battlements and gates. After that Victor wrote a letter to the Konchan gang.

"You cock-eyed Konchan blacksmiths that shod a mouse, we'll give you something to remember us by. We'll be waiting for you in our fort.

Victor Babkin,
Gymnasist, 2nd Class,
Commandant of the Fort."

They nailed the letter to a stick and Mishka Koryashonok took it to the village and stuck it into a snowdrift beside Artamon's cottage. Syomka, Lyonka and Artamoshka Junior, Alyoshka and Vanka Black Ears and Savoska's nephew Petrushka climbed on to the snowdrift beside the stick and for a long time hurled threats at the Konchan crowd, threw snowballs at them and then went away with Mishka Koryashonok and occupied the fort with him.

Victor ordered them to make snowballs of various sizes. They piled them up inside the fort walls, raised a flag-staff with a bunch of reeds on top of the turret and sat down to wait for the enemy.

Nikita came, looked at the fortifications and pushed his hands into his pockets.

"Nobody will come, your fort's no good; I'm not going to play with you, I'm going home."

"Found a girl to play with," shouted Victor over the wall. "Lady-killer!"

Artamon's boys laughed loudly, Vanka Black Ears whistled through his fingers.

"If I wanted to I'd chase the lot of you out of your fort," said Nikita, "only you're not worth dirtying my hands on," and he stuck his tongue out at Victor and went home across the pond.

Snowballs flew after him but he did not even turn round.

Those sitting in the fortress did not have long to wait: from the direction of the village, across the snow-covered backwaters, came the Konchan boys. They came straight towards the fortress, up to their knees in snow. There were about fifteen of them.

Victor began telling them that he would chop them all up for firewood and sniffed with his frost-reddened nose. He rolled his eyes. The Konchan boys stopped at the gates of the fort, some of them sat down on the snow. They had with them the little boy who wore his mother's shawl. The Konchan crowd was led by Styopka Karnaushkin. He took a good look at the fort and walked right up to the wall.

"Give us that boy with the shiny buttons," he said. "We'll rub his ears in the snow."

Victor sniffed with a troubled air. Mishka whispered, "Throw a lump of snow at him, heave it over!" Victor lifted up a lump of snow, threw it and missed. Karnaushkin stepped back to his own crowd. The Konchan boys jumped to their feet and began making snowballs.

52

Lumps of snow came flying at them from the fort. Artamon's boys were particularly good shots. They immediately knocked over the little boy in his mother's shawl. The Konchan boys began to reply. Clouds of snowballs flew from both sides. The pole with the device tied to it fell from the top of the turret.

Vanka Black Ears fell from the wall and surrendered to the Konchaners. Suddenly Victor's cap was knocked off and another snowball struck him in the face. The Konchan boys roared, howled and whistled, and charged into the fort. . . .

The wall was breached and the defenders fled through the reeds across the pond.

WHAT WAS IN THE VASE ON THE CLOCK

Nikita himself did not know why he found it dull playing with the boys. He went home, took off his hat and coat and as he walked through the rooms heard Lilya talking to her mother.

"Mamma, will you please give me a piece of clean rag. Valentina, my new doll, has hurt her leg and I'm worried about her health."

Nikita stood still and again felt the joy that he had known all those days. So great was his joy that it seemed as though a jolly music-box somewhere inside him was turning and playing a gentle tune.

Nikita went into the study, sat down on the sofa in the place where Lilya had sat two days before, screwed up his eyes and studied the frost-patterns on the windows. They were dainty and whimsical designs, designs from fairyland, from the place where the magic music-box was playing soundlessly. There were branches, leaves, trees and strange figures of animals and people. As he looked at the designs Nikita felt that words were putting themselves together and singing and that these astounding words and that singing gave him a tingling feeling on the crown of his head.

Nikita slid carefully off the sofa, looked for a small sheet of paper on his father's writing-desk and began to write verses in big letters:

> *Oh, my forest, you're my forest,*
> *You're my fairyland, my forest,*
> *You are full of beasts and birds,*
> *Wild men whisp'ring merry words,*
> *I love you, my forest,*
> *How I love my forest....*

It was too hard to write any more about the forest. Nikita chewed the end of the pen and looked up at the ceiling. Even the words that he had written were not those that had sung themselves spontaneously a short time before and had asked for their liberty. Nikita read through the poem and liked it all the same. He folded the paper in eight and put it in his pocket; he went into the dining-room where Lilya was sitting sewing by the window. The hand that held the paper in his pocket was damp with perspiration and somehow he could not make up his mind to show her the verses.

Victor came home at dusk, blue with the cold and with a swollen nose. Anna Apollosovna clapped her hands.

"They've broken his nose again! Whom have you been fighting with? Answer me this minute."

"I haven't been fighting with anybody, my nose swelled of itself," answered Victor gloomily; he went into his own room and lay down on the bed.

Nikita went in to him and stood beside the stove. A few stars had appeared in the greenish sky as though they had been pricked out with a needle.

"'Do you want me to read you a poem about the forest?" asked Nikita.

Victor shrugged his shoulders and put his feet on the bed-rail.

"You can tell that Styopka Karnaushkin that it will be better for him if he never comes near me again."

"D'you know," said Nikita, "this poem describes a certain forest. It's the sort of forest that you can't see but that everybody knows about. If you are miserable you read about that forest and you get better. Or, sometimes, you know, you see something in a dream that's awfully good, you don't know what it is but it's good—you wake up and you can't remember what it is ... understand?"

"No, I don't understand," said Victor, "and I don't want to listen to your poems."

Nikita sighed, stood a little while beside the stove and then went out. In the big hall that was lit up by the fire in the stove, Lilya was sitting on a trunk covered with a wolf-skin—she was watching the flames dancing in the fire.

Nikita sat down beside her on the trunk. The hall smelt of the heat of the stove, of the overcoats hanging there and there was the sweetly sad smell of old things in the huge chest of drawers.

"Let us talk a little," began Lilya thoughtfully, "tell me something interesting."

"Would you like me to tell you about a dream I saw not long ago?"

"Yes, tell me about the dream, please."

Nikita began to tell her the dream about the cat, the portraits that came to life, how he flew and what he saw when he was flying close to the ceiling. Lilya listened attentively, holding on her lap the doll whose leg had been bandaged.

55

When he had finished his story she turned to him and her eyes were open wide with fear and curiosity.

"What was in the vase?" she asked in a whisper.

"I don't know."

"There must have been something interesting there."

"But I saw it in a dream."

"It doesn't matter, you should have looked all the same. You're a boy, you don't understand anything. Tell me, have you really got a vase like that?"

"We've got a clock like that, but I don't remember the vase. The clock is in Grandad's study, it doesn't go."

"Let's go and have a look."

"It's dark there."

"We'll take a lantern from the Christmas tree. You bring the lantern, do, please."

Nikita ran into the drawing-room, took a lantern with coloured mica windows from the Christmas tree, lit it and went back to the hall.

Lilya threw a big woollen shawl round her shoulders. The children crept out into the corridor and slipped along to the summer rooms. In the dark high drawing-room there was a thick layer of frost on the windows and the moonlight threw the heavy black shadows of branches on to them. It was chilly and there was a smell of rotting apples. The oaken doors leading to the adjoining room were standing ajar.

"Is the clock in there?" asked Lilya.

"No, farther on, in the third room."

"Nikita, aren't you afraid of anything?"

Nikita pulled the door, it squeaked piteously and the sound echoed dully through the empty rooms. Lilya grasped Nikita by the arm. The lantern shivered and its red and yellow rays flickered on the walls.

The children entered the next room on tiptoe. Here the moonlight coming through the windows lay in bluish squares on the parquet floor.

There were striped armchairs against the walls and there in the corner was the bandy-legged sofa. Nikita's head was in a whirl—the room was exactly as he had once seen it.

"They're looking at us," whispered Lilya pointing to the two portraits on the wall—the old man and the old woman.

The children ran through the room and opened the other doors. The study was flooded with moonlight. The glass panes and their gilded frames in the doors of the bookcases were gleaming brightly. Over the fireplace, right in the light, the lady in the riding-habit smiled mysteriously.

"Who's that?" asked Lilya, coming close to Nikita.

"It's she," he answered in a whisper.

Lilya nodded, looked round the room and suddenly shouted: "The vase, look, Nikita, the vase!"

At the far end of the room stood a tall clock in a mahogany case, the disc of its pendulum hanging motionless: on top of the clock, between two wooden finials, stood a bronze vase decorated with the head of a lion. Somehow Nikita had never noticed it before but now he knew—that was the vase of his dream. He placed a chair against the clock, climbed on it and by standing on tiptoe reached into the vase: on the bottom he could feel dust and something hard.

"I've found it," he said, grasping it tight in his fist and jumping down to the floor. Just then something snorted at him from behind the bookcase, two violet eyes flashed and out darted the cat, Vasily Vasilievich, who was catching mice in the study.

Lilya waved her arms and ran. Nikita ran after her—he felt as though somebody's hand was touching his head, so awful it was. Vasily Vasilievich the cat overtook the children and ran silently through the moonlit rooms, his tail lowered.

The children ran into the hall and sat down again on the trunk scarcely able to get their breath from fear. Lilya's cheeks were burning.

"What is it?" she asked, looking Nikita straight in the eyes.

He opened his fingers. On the palm of his hand lay a thin ring with a blue stone in it. Lilya, speechless, clapped her hands.

"A ring!"

"It's a magic ring," said Nikita.

"Listen, what are we going to do with it?"

Nikita frowned, took her hand and began pushing the ring on to her index finger.

"No, why me?" asked Lilya; she looked at the stone, smiled, sighed and, throwing her arms round Nikita's neck, kissed him.

Nikita turned so red that he had to go away from the stove. He mustered all the courage he had and said:

"This is for you as well," and out of his pocket he pulled a piece of crumpled paper folded in eight, the paper on which he had written his poem, and gave it to Lilya.

She unfolded it, read it with her lips just moving, and then said pensively:

"Thank you, Nikita, I like your poem very much."

THE LAST EVENING

At tea that evening Mamma exchanged glances several times with Anna Apollosovna and shrugged her shoulders. Arkady Ivanovich sat gazing intently at his glass with a face that expressed nothing but gave you the idea that even if you killed him he wouldn't say a word. Anna Apollosovna finished her fifth cup of tea with cream and hot buns, cleared a space on the table in front of her of cups, plates and crumbs, and placed her big hand there, palm down.

"No, and no, and no, my dear Alexandra Leontievna," she said in her deep voice. "I never go back on what I have said: There's such a thing as too much of a good thing. So there you are, children,"—she turned round and dug Victor in the back with her forefinger so that he should not sit round-shouldered—"tomorrow is Monday, and that, of course, you've forgotten. Drink up your tea and go to bed immediately. We leave tomorrow morning at daybreak."

Victor silently pushed out his lips so that they protruded beyond the tip of his nose. Lilya quickly lowered her eyes and bent over her teacup. Nikita's eyes immediately became bleary and rays shot out from the flames of the lamp. He turned away and looked at Vasily Vasilievich.

The cat sat on the cleanly washed floor, busily licking a hind-leg that he held out like a pistol, his eyes screwed up. The cat was neither bored nor merry, there was nothing for him to hurry over; "tomorrow," he thought, "you people have a working day, you will again begin solving problems in arithmetic and writing dictation but I, the cat, have not celebrated any holidays, have not written any poems, have not kissed any girls, and my tomorrow will be all right."

Victor and Lilya finished their tea. Looking at their mother's thick brows that were already beginning to twitch they said goodnight and together with Nikita left the room.

"Victor!" Anna Apollosovna shouted after them.

"What, Mamma?"

"How are you walking?"

"What's the matter?"

"You're walking as though you were being pulled on a string. Walk smartly. Don't walk round the room in circles—that's the door, over there. Pull yourself up straight. . . . What you'll be fit for in life, I don't know!"

The children went out. In the warm and half-dark hall, where the boys had to turn to the right, Nikita stopped in front of Lilya and, biting his lips, said:

"Will you come and see us in the summer?"

"That depends on Mamma," answered Lilya in a thin voice, without raising her eyes.

"Will you write to me?"

"Yes, I'll write you letters, Nikita."

"Well, then, good-bye."

"Good-bye, Nikita."

Lilya tossed her hair-bow, held out her hand giving him the tips of her fingers and then went to her own room without turning back; she walked upright and precisely. You could not guess what she was thinking about as you watched her walk away. "A very, very reticent nature," Anna Apollosovna used to say.

While Victor was muttering to himself and packing his books and toys in a basket, unsticking and putting some pictures away in a little box, while he crawled under the table looking for his penknife, Nikita did not say a word: he undressed quickly, got into bed, covered his head with the blankets and pretended to be asleep.

He felt that the end of the world had come. As sleep overtook him he saw, like a shadow on the wall, a huge hair-bow that he would never forget for the rest of his life. In his sleep he heard voices, somebody came over to his bed, then the voices drew farther away again. He saw warm branches like arms, huge trees, a reddish path through thick undergrowth that opened up easily before him. It was uncommonly pleasant in that strange forest, reddish from the light and he wanted to cry on account of something sadder than he had ever known before. Suddenly a red Indian wearing golden spectacles stuck his head out between the leaves. "Oh, you're still sleeping," shouted the head in a voice of thunder.

Nikita opened his eyes. The warm morning light fell on his face. In front of the bed stood Arkady Ivanovich tapping his nose with the end of a pencil.

"Get up, get up, you young brigand!"

SEPARATION

At the end of January Vasily Nikitievich, Nikita's father, sent a letter home.

"... I am in despair, the business with the legacy seems to be going to keep me for a long time yet, my dear Sasha—apparently I shall have to go to Moscow for the business. In any case I shall be with you by Lent...."

The letter made Mamma very sad and in the evening she showed it to Arkady Ivanovich.

"I've had enough of that legacy business," she said. "I don't want it if it causes so much trouble; we've been separated the whole winter. Sometimes I think that Nikita has even begun to forget his father."

She turned away and stared at the black, frosted window. It was black outside and the frost was so heavy that the trees in the garden crackled, the roof beams in the attic creaked so loudly that the whole house shook and in the mornings they would find dead sparrows lying on the snow. Mamma dabbed her eyes with her handkerchief.

"Yes, separation, separation," muttered Arkady Ivanovich and was apparently thinking about his own separation—his hand fumbled for a letter in his pocket.

At the moment Nikita was drawing a map of South America—his mother had had a long talk with him that day, she grew angry and told him that during the holidays he had become lazy and had let himself go, that apparently he wanted to become a provincial clerk or a telegraph operator at Bezenchuk Station. "Instead of silly pictures," she said, "you'll draw me a map of South America this evening."

Nikita drew the map of America but all the time he was wondering whether he had really forgotten his father. No. In place of the Amazon, at the point where the lines of latitude and longitude crossed, he saw his father's face,—rosy cheeks, flashing eyes and flashing teeth,

61

a jolly face with a dark beard parted in two and a loud laughing voice. You could sit for hours staring at his mouth and die from laughter over his stories. Mamma frequently accused him of irresponsibility and frivolity but actually he had a rather too lively character. Suddenly, for example, his father would get the idea that the frogs that filled the three ponds on the estate were all going to waste and would sit for evenings talking about how to feed them, breed them, salt them down in barrels and send them to Paris. "You can laugh," he would say to Mamma, whose laughter over the whole business brought tears to her eyes, "but you'll see how much money I earn with the frogs." Father ordered part of a pond to be fenced off and frog-pens made, he boiled a mash to feed them on, and brought experimental frogs into the house until Mamma said that he could either have the frogs or her, that she was scared to death of them and that the idea of living in a house full of frogs disgusted her.

One day Father went to town and from there sent back carts loaded with old oak doors and window-frames. His letter said: "Dear Sasha, quite by accident I managed to buy up a lot of window-frames and doors cheaply. These are just what we need for the pavilion you dreamed of building on the hill under the poplars. I have spoken to an architect who recommends building a pavilion that we can live in during the winter if we want to. I am quite taken up with the idea because our house stands in such a hollow that there's no sort of view from the windows." Mamma only cried: for three months Arkady Ivanovich's salary had not been paid and now he had undertaken fresh expenses.... She flatly refused to have the pavilion built and the window-frames and doors stood rotting in a shed. Then Father got another fever—agricultural improvements—and again a dead loss: he ordered machinery from America, brought it from the station himself, grew angry teaching the workers to handle it and shouted at everybody, "Careful, careful, you accursed devils!"

Some time later Mamma asked:

"Well, and what about your wonderful binder?"

"What about it?" Father drummed with his fingers on the window-pane. "It's a fine machine."

"I saw it. It's standing in the shed."

Father shrugged his shoulders and rapidly stroked his beard in two parts.

"Is it broken?" asked Mamma.

"Those fools of Americans," snorted Father, "think up machines that break every minute. It's not my fault."

As he drew the Amazon and its tributaries Nikita thought of his father with love and a tender pleasure. His conscience was clear, his mother had made a mistake in saying he had forgotten his father.

Suddenly something in the wall cracked like a pistol-shot. Mamma gasped loudly and dropped her knitting on the floor. Under the chest of drawers Akhilka, the hedgehog, grunted and snorted in anger. Nikita looked at Arkady Ivanovich, who pretended to be reading, but his eyes were closed although he was not asleep. Nikita was sorry for Arkady Ivanovich: the poor fellow was always thinking about his fiancée, Vassa Nilovna, a school-teacher in the town. That's what separation means!

Nikita rested his cheek in his hand and began to think about his own separation. Lilya had sat at this same table and now she was no longer there. How sad—there she was and now she was gone. There was the stain on the table where she had spilled the gum. And on that wall the shadow of her hair-bow had often fallen. "Happy days have flown away." Nikita's throat ached from these extraordinarily sad words that he had just thought of. In order not to forget them he wrote them down under the map of America: "Happy days have flown away." He continued drawing and took the Amazon where it did not belong—all through Paraguay and Uruguay to Tierra del Fuego.

"Alexandra Leontievna, I'm afraid you're right: that boy's training to be a telegraphist at Bezenchuk Station," said Arkady Ivanovich in that cold, calm voice that gave you the creeps; for a long time he had been looking at what Nikita was doing to the map.

WORKADAY WORLD

The frosts became fiercer. Icy winds shook the hoar-frost from the trees. The snow was covered with a hard crust over which the frozen and hungry wolves, single and in pairs, came right up to the estate at night.

When they smelt the wolves Sharok and Katok would begin to whine, crawl under the coach-house and from there howl in tones that cut right through you, "Oo-oo-oo-ooo."

The wolves crossed the frozen pond and stood in the reeds sniffing the smells of human habitation. They grew bolder and came into the garden, sat down on the glade in front of the house, stared at the dark, frozen windows with their flashing eyes, raised their heads into the frozen darkness and began on a low note as though growling, then louder and louder, raising their hungry call higher and higher, they began to howl, continuously, higher and higher, penetratingly....

These wolf howls made Sharok and Katok bury their heads in the straw and lay senseless with fear under the coach-house. In the workers' quarters the carpenter Pakhom, tossing on the stove under his long, sheepskin greatcoat, muttered half asleep:

"Oh, Lord, how heavy are our sins!"

These were working-days in the house. Everybody got up early, when the crimson light of dawn had just reached the bluish-black windows, the frost-bound windows became a little brighter and there was light in the upper part of the room.

Stove doors clanged in the house. In the kitchen the tin oil-lamp was still burning. There was the smell of a samovar and of warm bread. They did not sit long over breakfast. Mamma cleared the table in the dining-room and got out the sewing-machine. A seamstress came to them from the village of Pestravka—bent, pockmarked Sonya, with a front tooth worn down from constant biting of thread; together with Mamma she stitched all sorts of everyday things. They spoke in low voices over their sewing, they ripped calico with a crackling sound. Sonya the seamstress had a dull, uninteresting look about her, and seemed to have been lying behind a cupboard for years, to have just been found, cleaned up a little and set to sew.

These days Arkady Ivanovich was more pressing with the studies and made, as he loved to say, a leap forward: they made a start on algebra, a subject that is as dry as dust.

While learning arithmetic it is possible to think of all sorts of useless but interesting things: about rusty tanks with dead mice in them into which water poured through three pipes, or about the eternal "someone" in an oilcloth coat with a long nose who mixed three sorts of coffee or bought so many ingots of copper or that same unlucky merchant with his two pieces of cloth. But in algebra there was nothing to take hold of, there was no living thing in it, the only interesting thing was that the binding of the book smelled of glue and when Arkady Ivanovich bent over Nikita's chair to explain the rules his face, round like a water-jug, was reflected in the ink-well.

When Arkady Ivanovich talked about history he stood with his back to the stove. The reflection of his black frock-coat, ginger beard and gold spectacles in the white tiles was simply marvellous. He was telling Nikita how Pepin the Short at Soissons hacked through a mug and Arkady Ivanovich brought his arm down with a sweep to cut the air with his hand.

"You must get this into your head," he said to Nikita. "People like Pepin the Short were famous for their unwavering will power and courage. Unlike some people, they were not too lazy to work, they did not let their eyes wander to the ink-well in which nothing is written, they did not even know such shameful words as 'I can't' or 'I'm tired.' They did not twist the hair on their foreheads instead of mastering the rules of algebra. That's why," he raised the book which he held with a finger between the pages, "they serve as examples to us today."

After lunch Mamma usually said to Arkady Ivanovich:

"If it's twenty degrees below again today, Nikita cannot go out."

Arkady Ivanovich walked to the window and breathed on the glass at the place where the thermometer was hanging outside.

"Twenty-one and a half, Alexandra Leontievna."

"I thought so," said Mamma, "go and find something to do, Nikita."

Nikita went into his father's study, climbed on to the leather sofa at the end nearest the stove and opened a magic book by Fenimore Cooper.

It was so quiet in the study that a scarcely audible ringing sound began in his ears. What wonderful stories one could think up when one was alone with that sound on the sofa. White light streamed through the frosty windows. Nikita read Cooper: then, lying for a long time with his brows knitted, he imagined waves of green grass rustling in the wind over the wide prairies that had no beginning and no end; piebald mustangs turned their merry heads towards him and neighed at full gallop; dark canyons; a grey waterfall and above it the Chief of the Hurons standing motionless in his war bonnet on a high crag shaped like a sugar-loaf, a long rifle in his hand. In the depths of a forest, on a stone between the roots of a giant tree, he,

Nikita himself, sat with his fists pressed into his cheeks. A fire burned at his feet. It was so quiet in the forest that he could hear ringing in his ears. Nikita had come in search of Lilya who had been cunningly kidnapped. He performed many brave deeds, carried Lilya on a wild mustang on many occasions, scrambled through the canyons and with a skilful shot brought the Chief of the Hurons down from the sugar-loaf crag but each time he shot him down the Chief got up on the rock again; Nikita kidnapped and saved Lilya and just had to keep on saving and kidnapping her.

When the frost and Mamma allowed him to poke his nose out of doors Nikita wandered about the yard alone. The games he used to play with Mishka Koryashonok bored him and Mishka nowadays spent most of his time in the workers' quarters playing cards—at "nose" or at "khlyust," a game in which the loser was dragged along by his hair.

Nikita went over to the well and remembered: from here he had seen at the window of the house the only blue hair-bow in the world. The window was empty now. Over by the coach-house Sharok and Katok had dug a dead jackdaw out of the snow—it was the same jackdaw: stooping down beside it Lilya had said, "What a pity, Nikita, look, a dead bird." Nikita took the jackdaw away from the dogs, carried it beyond the cellars and buried it in a snowdrift.

As he crossed the dam Nikita remembered how he had walked that way on the night after the Christmas party under the huge willows that were transparent in the moonlight and how his shadow slipped along by his side. Why was it that he had not at that time sufficiently valued that which had happened to him? That was the time when he should have closed his eyes and have felt keenly how great was his happiness. Now a biting wind was howling through the frozen, black willows; on the pond the ice ramp from which he and Lilya had raced on their toboggan had grown smaller—he remembered that Lilya had not spoken, had screwed up her eyes and held tightly on to the sides of the toboggan. All traces of that lay buried under the snow.

Nikita walked over a good hard snow crust out of the yard where to the north the snowdrifts were level with the thatched roofs. From here he could see the whole flat white field, a snow desert that merged in frosty gloom with the sky. A whirlwind trailed across the snow like a column of smoke. The skirts of his sheepskin coat were blown back. Powdered snow blew from the crest of a snowdrift. Nikita himself did not know why he wanted to stand and gaze at the desert of snow.

Mamma had begun to notice that Nikita was walking about looking miserable and she spoke of it to Arkady Ivanovich. They decided to stop the algebra lessons, to send Nikita to bed early and, as Arkady Ivanovich not very wittily expressed it, "pump him out" with castor oil, all of which was done.

Arkady Ivanovich noticed that Nikita became happier. The real cure, however, came three weeks later: it was a strong wind from the south that rolled a grey mist over the fields, orchards and garden and was accompanied by tattered clouds that raced madly across the sky.

ROOKS

In the workers' quarters on Sunday, the labourer Vasily, Mishka Koryashonok, Leksya the shepherd boy, and Artyom, a tall bony man with a long crooked nose, were playing cards. Artyom had been day-labourer all his life, he had always wanted to marry but the girls would not have him. Some short time before he had begun to take notice of Dunyasha, a pretty, rosy-cheeked girl who looked after the dairy. All day long she ran back and forth from the cowshed to the cellars or the kitchen, her galvanized iron pails clanging; she always smelt of fresh milk and when she went out the snowflakes seemed to sparkle on her cheeks. She was a girl full of laughter. Wherever Artyom was—whether he was carrying bran from the barns or cleaning out the sheep-pens—if he saw Dunyasha, he would stick his pitchfork into the ground and go after her, walking on his long legs with the gait of a camel.

Going up to Dunyasha he would take off his cap and bow.

"Good-morning, Dunyasha."

"Good-morning." Dunyasha would put down her pails and cover her mouth with the corner of her apron.

"Still running about with the milk, Dunyasha?"

Then Dunyasha would stoop down —it was so funny she could not stand it any longer—pick up the pails and run along the icy path to the cellar where she would drop the pails on the floor with a bang; in her rapid patter she told the housekeeper, Vasilisa: "That camel is again asking me to marry him. O-oh dear, he'll be the death of me!" and she laughed so merrily that she could be heard all over the yard.

Nikita went into the workers' quarters. Today they were making a stew of sheep's-heads and there was a fine smell of boiled mutton and freshly baked bread. At the door, where an earthenware water-jug with a spout hung over a water-butt, there lay grey snow brought in from the street. Pakhom sat on a bench by the stove, his black hair falling on to his pockmarked forehead and his frowning brows. He was stitching the shaft of a boot: with his bradawl he carefully pierced the hole in the leather, held back his head, squinted, threaded a hog bristle on to his wax end, stabbed it into the hole and grasping the boot shaft tightly between his knees pulled the thread through in both directions. He looked frowningly at Nikita for he was very angry: today he had quarrelled with the cook who had hung his foot-cloths up to dry and had burned them.

The card players sat at the table in their clean Sunday shirts, their heads neatly oiled and combed. Only Artyom wore a ragged homespun jacket and had not combed his hair: there was nobody to look after him and wash his shirts. The card players slammed their sticky, smelly cards down on the table, shouting:

"That's ten to you."

"And fifty for you."

"D'you see that?"

"And what about that?"

"Game!"

"Eh?"

"Hold your nose out, Artyom."

"Why me?" asked Artyom, looking at the cards in astonishment. "That's wrong, it's a mistake."

"Hold out your nose."

Artyom took a card in each hand and covered his eyes with them.

The labourer, Vasily, took three cards and began to hit slowly at Artyom's long nose with them. The other players watched Artyom, counted the blows and told him angrily not to budge.

Nikita sat down to play with them, immediately lost a game and got fifteen blows on the nose. Just then Pakhom, placing the boot shaft and the bradawl under the bench, said sternly:

"Some people would be coming back from mass now but these don't even bother to cross their foreheads—they go straight to the cards. Before we know where we are they'll be eating meat during Lent.... Stepanida!" he shouted, getting up and going towards the water-jug, "get dinner ready!"

In the kitchen, Stepanida, the cook, was so scared that she dropped a saucepan lid. The workers gathered up the cards, Vasily turned towards the corner where there was a paper icon covered with the marks of black beetles and began to cross himself.

Stepanida brought in a wooden bowl with sheep's-heads in it: the cook turned her head away as the fragrant steam that rose from the dish enveloped her head. The workers sat down to table silently and serious-ly, taking a spoon each. Vasily began cutting bread into long slices, gave a slice to each of the workers and then rapped on the wooden bowl with a spoon and they all fell to. The sheep's-head stew was good.

Pakhom did not sit down with the others, he merely took a piece of bread and returned to the bench by the stove. The cook brought him some boiled potatoes and a wooden salt-cellar. He was observing the Lenten fast.

"Footcloths," Pakhom said to her, carefully breaking a steaming potato in two and dipping a half into the salt-cellar. "You burnt the footcloths, again I say you're an old hag, again I say you're a fool. And that's that...."

Nikita went out into the yard. It was a dull day. A heavy wet wind was blowing. Horse dung had begun to show through, giving the grey

snow, powdery like salt, a yellowish tinge. The sleigh road that turned towards the dam, covered with dung and with numerous puddles on it, was higher than the surrounding snow-field. The log walls of the sheds and barns, the blackened straw thatch, the big, unpainted timber house, everything was black, grey and clearly defined.

Nikita walked over to the dam. From the distance he could hear the rustling of the wet trees, so loud that it seemed as though water were pouring through sluice-gates some distance away. The swaying crowns of the willows were hidden in the low, flying, tattered clouds. In the clouds, amongst the waving branches, black birds were flying round in circles and screeching with hoarse alarmed cries.

Nikita stood there with his head thrown back and his mouth open. These birds seemed to have come out of the heavy, wet wind, they seemed to have been carried along with the clouds, and hanging on to the noisy rocking willows they screamed about turbulent, fearful and happy times; Nikita held his breath and his heart beat faster.

These were the rooks that flew back to their old places, to their damaged nests, with the first spring storm. Spring had come.

THE HOUSE ON WHEELS

The wet wind blew for three days, eating away the snow. On the higher places patches of black ploughland showed through the snow. The air smelled of thawing snow, of horse dung and cattle. When the doors of the cowshed were opened the cows went down to the well pressing close against each other, clashing their horns and lowing loudly. The bull Bayan roared savagely as he smelled the spring wind. Mishka Koryashonok and Leksya with their whips drove the cattle back into sheds that smelled of dung. They opened the doors of the stables and the horses came out sleepily as though they were drunk, their coats dark and moulting, their manes long and tangled and their bellies distended. Vesta was foaling in a loose-box beside the stable. Wet jackdaws, bustling about aimlessly and screaming, flew over the roofs. Round at the back, behind the cellars, the crows crowded round some carrion that had appeared from under the snow. The trees were noisy, noisy with a harsh, menacing sound. In the trees and clouds over the dam the rooks cawed as they flew about.

Nikita had a headache during all these days. Sleepy and worried he wandered about the yard, along the water-swollen roads, went to the threshing barns where the broken stacks of chaff smelt of grain dust and mice. He was vaguely troubled as though something awful were going to happen, something that could be neither understood nor forgiven. Everything—the earth, wild beasts, cattle, birds—was no longer friendly and understandable to him, they had been alienated, were hostile and malicious. Something was about to happen, something incomprehensible, so sinful that you could die. Nevertheless, sleepy and made dizzy by the wind, the smell of carrion, the horses' hoofs, the dung and the crumbling snow, he was bothered by a curiosity that drew him on to what was happening around him.

When he returned home wet, wild-looking and smelling of dogs his mother looked at him attentively, without any tenderness and with a look of condemnation. He did not know what had made her angry and this oppressed him still more; it worried Nikita. During the past few days he had done nothing bad but still felt anxious as though he were guilty of some great sin that for no apparent reason was sweeping across the whole earth.

Nikita walked along the windward side of the strawstack. In this stack there were still the holes that the workers and the girls had dug out in the autumn when they were threshing the last of the wheat. At night the people would creep into the holes and caves to sleep. Nikita remembered the talk he had heard in the darkness under the warm, smelly straw. The stack seemed a terrible place.

Nikita walked on to the ploughmen's booth that stood near the threshing barn, a little plank house on wheels. The door of the caravan, hanging from one hinge, creaked dismally in the wind. The caravan was empty. Nikita entered it by the little five-rung ladder. It had a little window with four tiny panes of glass. There was still snow lying on the floor. On the shelf that ran along one wall high up under the roof lay a gnawed wooden spoon that had been there since the previous autumn, a bottle that had held vegetable oil and the handle of a knife. The wind howled over the roof. Nikita stood there and thought that now he was alone and forlorn, that nobody loved him, that everybody was angry with him. Everything in the world was wet, black and evil. His eyes grew moist, he was very sorry for himself: why should he not be—alone in all the world, in an empty booth....

"Lord," said Nikita in a low voice and cold shivers immediately ran down his back, "Oh, Lord, let everything be good again. Let Mamma love me, let me obey Arkady Ivanovich.... Let the sun come out and the grass grow.... Let the rooks not scream so terribly,....

Let me not hear how Bayan the bull roars. . . . Lord, let things be good again for me. . . ."

As Nikita said these words he bowed his head and hurriedly crossed himself. When he had finished his prayer, looking up at the wooden spoon, the oil bottle and the knife handle, he really did feel easier. He stood for a little while longer in that little house with the tiny window and then went back home.

The little house really had helped. As he was taking his coat off in the entrance-hall, his mother looked at him as she passed in the way she always looked at him nowadays—attentively with her severe grey eyes—and suddenly smiled tenderly and passed her hand over Nikita's head.

"Well, have you run about long enough?" she asked. "Do you want your tea?"

THE UNEXPECTED APPEARANCE
OF VASILY NIKITIEVICH

That night the rain came at last, a real downpour that beat so heavily on the window and the iron roof that Nikita awoke, sat up in bed and smiled.

The rain had a wonderful sound at night. "Sleep, sleep, sleep," it drummed against the glass and in the darkness the wind tore at the poplar-trees in front of the house.

Nikita turned his pillow over, cold side up, lay down again and turned and twisted under the knitted woollen blanket until he had made himself comfortable. "Everything will be terribly, terribly good," he thought and dropped down into the soft warm clouds of sleep.

In the morning it had stopped raining but the sky was laden with heavy wet clouds that were floating from south to north. Nikita looked out of the window and gasped. Not a trace of the snow was left. The extensive yard was covered with blue puddles that were ruffled by the wind. The sleigh track stretched through the puddles, across the flattened brown grass and had not yet completely disappeared. The soaking wet lavender-coloured branches of the poplars were shaking with lively joy. From the south a patch of dazzling-blue sky appeared through the torn clouds and with terrific speed flew towards the house.

At breakfast Mamma was worried and kept looking at the windows.

"This is the fifth day we've had no mail," she said to Arkady Ivanovich, "I don't know why.... Now the floods have come and the roads will be impassable for another fortnight.... Such thoughtlessness is terrible."

Nikita realized that Mamma was talking about his father whom they expected to arrive any day. Arkady Ivanovich went to talk with the steward and find out whether it would be possible to send a horseman for the mail, but immediately returned to the dining-room and spoke in a loud voice that had unusual tones in it.

"Oh, Lord, what is happening! ... Go out and listen to the noise the water is making."

Nikita threw open the doors leading to the porch. The whole sharp, fresh air was filled with the strong soft sound of falling water. The sound came from the countless streams of thawed snow that ran along furrows, ditches and canals into the gullies. Gullies filled to the brim carried the spring waters to the river. Breaking through the ice the river overflowed its banks, and twirling ice-floes and bushes torn up by the roots, was racing along high over the dam and down into the millpools.

The azure patch that had flown over the house burst and drove away all the clouds; a cold blue light lit up the sky, turning the pools in the yard a deep, bottomless blue; there were flashing reflections in the rivulets and the huge lakes in the fields and the brimming gullies all reflected the sun in rays of light.

"Good God, what wonderful air," said Mamma pressing her hands to her breast under her woollen shawl. Her face was smiling and there were green flashes in her grey eyes. When she smiled, Mamma was more beautiful than anybody else on earth.

Nikita went round the yard to see what was happening there. There were rivulets everywhere, some of them disappearing under the grey, crumbling snowdrifts that sighed and collapsed when you put your foot on them. No matter which way you went there was water everywhere: the house was like an island. Nikita only managed to get as far as the smithy which stood on a low hill. Down an already drying slope he ran to the gully. Sweeping over the grass of last year the clear, fragrant snow-water raced along. He picked up a handful and drank it.

Farther down the gully the snow still lay in yellow and blue patches. In some places the water cut through the patches in a stream, in others it flowed over the top of the snow. God help anybody who got caught in one of these patches of snow much with a horse. Nikita walked along the grass beside the gully: he thought how good it would be to swim in the spring waters from gully to gully past the drying but still soggy banks and across the big glittering lakes whose surfaces were ruffled by the spring wind.

On the far side of the gully lay a level field, brown in some places, still snow-covered in others, all sparkling with the ruffled surface of

77

its many rivulets. In the distance five horsemen were slowly crossing the field on unsaddled horses. The leader turned round and apparently shouted something to the others, waving a coil of rope. Nikita knew by the piebald horse that the rider was Artamon Tyurin. The last rider held a long pole over his shoulder. The horsemen rode on towards Khomyakovka, a village that lay on the far side of the river beyond the gullies. It was very strange to see the men riding across the flooded fields where there was no visible road.

Nikita went down to the lower pond into which the gully poured its wide foaming waters over the yellow snow. The water covered the whole ice of the pond, travelling in little waves. To the left the willows, thawed out, bushy and huge, were rustling noisily. The rooks, wet from the night's rain, sat amongst the bare swaying branches.

A horseman appeared on the dam amongst the twisted trunks of the willows. His heels were beating away at the sides of a sorry nag, he rolled in his seat and flapped his elbows up and down. It was Styopka Karnaushkin, he shouted something to Nikita as he galloped past across the pools of water; lumps of muddy snow and splashes of water flew from the hoofs of his horse.

Obviously something had happened. Nikita ran to the house. By the back porch, its sides pumping, stood Karnaushkin's nag; it tossed its head at Nikita. He ran into the house just in time to hear his mother's short, loud shriek of fear. She appeared from the end of the corridor, her face distorted, her eyes dilated with terror. Styopka appeared behind her and Arkady Ivanovich came running out of a door on the other side. Mamma did not walk but flew down the corridor.

"Hurry, hurry," she cried, throwing open the kitchen door, "Stepanida, Dunyasha, run to the workers' quarters! Vasily Nikitievich is drowning near Khomyakovka...."

The worst thing of all was that it was "near Khomyakovka." Everything went black before Nikita's eyes: the passage was suddenly filled with the smell of fried onions. Mamma said afterwards that Nikita screwed up his eyes and screamed like a rabbit. He did not remember that scream, however. Arkady Ivanovich grabbed hold of him and took him into the class-room.

"Aren't you ashamed of yourself, Nikita, a big lad like you," he kept repeating, squeezing Nikita's two arms just above the elbow. "What about it, what about it? Vasily Nikitievich will be coming soon.... He's obviously fallen into a ditch and got a soaking.... And that idiot of a Styopka has scared your mother.... On my word of honour I'll pull his ears off...."

Still Nikita could see that Arkady Ivanovich's lips were twitching and that the pupils of his eyes had narrowed to pinpoints.

In the meantime Mamma, wearing only her shawl, had run to the workers' quarters although the workers already knew and were at the coach-house fussing about trying to harness the big, strong, bad-tempered stallion Nero to a flat-bottomed sleigh; in the horse pasture they caught riding-horses; one man was pulling a long-handled boat-hook down from the thatched roof, another ran up with a spade, another with a coil of rope; Dunyasha ran out of the house, her arms filled with a long sheepskin greatcoat and a heavy fur coat. Pakhom went up to Mamma.

"Pull yourself together, Alexandra Leontievna, send Dunyasha to the village for vodka. As soon as we bring him give him the vodka to drink...."

"Pakhom, I'm coming with you...."

"Not for anything, go home, you'll catch cold."

Pakhom sat sideways in the sleigh and took a firm hold of the reins. "Let him go!" he shouted to the boys who held the bridle. Nero plunged in the shafts, snorted, took off with a jerk and easily pulled the sleigh over the mud and puddles. The workers followed in a close group behind him flogging their horses with ropes.

Mamma stood still for a long time looking after them, then walked slowly back to the house with her head bowed. Mamma sat down at the window of the dining-room from which the open field was visible and, away beyond the hills, the tops of the willows of Khomyakovka; she sent for Nikita. He ran in, threw his arms round her neck and leaned his head against the woollen shawl over her shoulders. . . .

"God protect us from all misfortune, Nikita dear," said Mamma softly and pressed her lips hard and long against Nikita's hair.

Arkady Ivanovich came into the room several times, adjusted his glasses and rubbed his hands. Several times Mamma went out on to the porch to see whether they were coming yet, returned to the window and did not let Nikita leave her side.

The daylight had already turned to a faint lavender before sunset, the lower parts of the window-panes were covered with light frost patterns for it was cold at night. Quite suddenly they heard the beat of a horse's hoofs right outside the house and they saw Nero with a foam-flecked mouth, Pakhom sitting sideways on the edge of the sleigh and in the sleigh itself, under a pile composed of the sheepskin greatcoat, the fur coat and a piece of felt they could distinguish the red, smiling face of Vasily Nikitievich peeping out from the sheepskin; in place of a moustache he had two enormous icicles. Mamma cried out, jumped up and her face was twitching.

"He's alive!" she cried and the tears flowed from her sparkling eyes.

HOW I ALMOST DROWNED

Father sat in a huge leather armchair that had been pulled up to the round table in the dining-room. Vasily Nikitievich was dressed in a soft camel-hair dressing-gown and soft felt boots. His moustaches and his damp chestnut beard had been combed in two parts and his merry red face was reflected in the samovar; the samovar, like everything else that evening, had something special about the way it bubbled and spat sparks out of the grill below.

Vasily Nikitievich sat with his eyes screwed up with pleasure and with the vodka he had drunk, and his white teeth showed up with great brilliance. Although Mamma was still wearing the same plain grey dress and the woollen shawl she seemed quite different, not a bit like herself—she could not hold back her smiles, her lips wrinkled and her chin trembled. Arkady Ivanovich had put on his new tortoise-shell glasses that he kept for special occasions. Nikita knelt on a chair, his stomach pressed against the table, and was breathlessly listening to his father. Every minute Dunyasha ran in and out, took something,

brought something and stared at the master. Stepanida brought in some special fried cakes in a heavy cast-iron frying-pan and as they stood on the table they sizzled in the butter looking delicious. Vasily Vasilievich the cat, his tail held up straight, walked back and forth and round and round the leather armchair, rubbing his back, his sides and his head

against it, purring merrily and unnaturally loudly. The pig's snout of Akhilka the hedgehog peeped out from under the sideboard, his needles lay flat on his back showing that he was also glad.

Father ate a hot cake with great satisfaction—"Good old Stepanida!"—took another, rolled it up in a tube and ate that too—"Good old Stepanida!"—took a long sip of tea with cream, stroked his moustaches and screwed up one eye.

"Now let me tell you how I almost drowned," and he began to tell his story. "I left Samara the day before yesterday. It's like this, Sasha," for a moment he was serious, "I had made a very profitable purchase: that Pozdyunin kept worrying me to buy his dark-bay stallion, Byron. 'What do I want your stallion for?' I asked him. 'Come and look at it,' he said. I saw the stallion and took a liking to it. A beauty. Smart, too. He looked at me with his violet eyes and almost said, 'Buy me.' And Pozdyunin kept after me all the time to buy the horse. And he had a sleigh and harness as well. . . . Sasha, you're not angry with me for making that purchase, are you?" Father took mother's hand in his. "Forgive me." Mamma even closed her eyes— how could she be angry today even if he had bought Pozdyunin, the chairman of the Zemstvo, himself. "So I ordered Byron to be brought to me and then wondered what I should do with him. I didn't want to leave the horse alone in Samara. I packed a lot of presents into a bag," Father closed one eye roguishly, "Byron was harnessed for me at dawn and I left Samara alone. At first there was still snow left in some places but soon the whole road was so washed out that my stallion was all of a lather and he began to stagger. I decided to spend the night in Koldyban with Father Vozdvizhensky. The priest treated me to some sausage—just marvellous! All right, then. The priest said, 'Vasily Nikitievich, you can't get home, you'll see—the ice on the gullies is certain to break tonight.' But I had made up my mind to go whatever happened. And so I argued with the priest till midnight. He gave me such a wonderful black-currant wine! Upon my word, if you took such a liqueur to Paris the French would be crazy about it.... We'll speak about that later, though. I went to bed and then it began raining cats and dogs. You can imagine how miserable that made me feel, Sasha: there I was, twenty versts away from you and did not know when I should be able to reach you.... I'd had enough of the rain and the priest and the wine...."

"Vasily," Mamma interrupted him and began looking at him severely, "I ask you very seriously never to take such risks again."

"I promise I won't, upon my word," said Vasily Nikitievich without pausing to think. "And so.... By morning the rain had stopped, the priest went to mass, I ordered Byron to be harnessed and drove off. Good Lord! There was nothing but water all round me. But it was easier going for the stallion. We had to travel without roads, knee-deep in water, across lakes.... Wonderful.... Sun, wind.... My sleigh was floating, my feet were wet. It was so good! At last I saw our willows in the distance. I passed Khomyakovka and started looking for the easiest place to cross the river.... The scoundrel!" Vasily Nikitievich struck his fist on the arm of the chair. "I'll show that Pozdyunin where bridges have to be built! I had to drive about three versts beyond Khomyakovka and then ford the river. He's a fine horse, Byron, pulled me straight up the steep bank. When the river was behind me I thought of the three gullies ahead, they'd be worse. There was no way back. I drove up to the first gully. Just imagine it, Sasha, the water mixed with snow was level with the banks. The gully, you know, is about fifteen feet deep."

"Dreadful," said Mamma, turning pale.

"I unharnessed the stallion, took off the collar and saddle pad and put them in the sleigh but I did not think to take my fur coat off— that was the cause of all the trouble. I climbed on to Byron's back—

God bless me! The stallion jibbed at first. I stroked him. He smelled the water and snorted. He stumbled and then plunged into the gully, straight into the snow mush. He sank up to his neck and began to flounder but could not budge an inch. I climbed down and also sank in the mush, only my head sticking out. I began twisting round in the mush, sort of half swimming, half crawling. The stallion saw that I was going away from him and he began neighing pitifully—don't leave me—he worked with his feet and crawled after me. He caught me up and his fore hoofs got entangled in the skirts of my open coat and dragged me into the water. I fought with all my strength but was dragged down deeper and deeper and there was no bottom under my feet. It was lucky the coat was unbuttoned and when 1 was struggling under the water the coat slipped off. It's still there on the bottom of the gully. I came to the surface, began to breathe again and lay spread-eagled on the mush like a frog; I heard a bubbling noise, looked round and saw that half the stallion's head was under water and bubbles were coming up from his nose—he had stepped on the reins. I had to return to him. I unfastened the buckle and tore the reins free. He turned his head and looked at me like a human being. We floundered for something like an hour in that mush. I felt that I had no more strength and was beginning to freeze. My heart began to grow cold. Just then I noticed that the stallion had stopped treading water, he had turned and was swimming—that meant we'd reached open water. It was easier to swim in the water and we were cast up on the far bank. Byron got out first on to the grass and I followed him. I caught hold of his mane and we walked along side by side, both of us swaying. In front of us there were two more gullies.... Then I saw the men riding towards us...."

Vasily Nikitievich said a few more indistinct words and suddenly dropped his head. His face was scarlet, his teeth were chattering.

"It's nothing, it's nothing, your samovar has gassed me," he said, leaned back in his chair and closed his eyes.

The shivers began. He was put to bed in a delirium. . . .

PASSION WEEK

Father lay for three days in a fever and then came to himself; the first thing he asked was whether Byron was alive. The beautiful stallion was in the best of health.

Vasily Nikitievich's lively and jolly character soon had him on his feet again: this was not the time to lie in bed. The busy time preceding the spring sowing had began. In the smithy they were putting edges on the ploughshares and mending ploughs, shoeing all the horses. In the barns workers were shovelling over the musty grain, frightening the mice and raising clouds of dust. Under a shed the winnowing-machine was whirring. In the house spring cleaning was well under way: windows were cleaned, floors washed, cobwebs swept down from the ceilings. The carpets, chairs and sofas were taken out on the balcony and the spirit of winter was beaten out of them. All the things that had become accustomed to lying in their own places during the winter were moved, cleaned of dust and newly arranged. Akhilka, who hated any bustle, was so angry that he went to sleep in a storeroom.

Mamma herself cleaned the dining-room silver and the silver frames of the icons, opened the old chests, filling the air with a smell of moth-balls, looked over the spring clothes that had been crushed in the chests but seemed like new from having been laid up during the winter. In the dining-room there was a basket of hard-boiled eggs; Nikita and Arkady Ivanovich coloured them with a decoction of onion skins which made them yellow, wrapped them up in paper and dropped them into boiling water with vinegar which gave the eggs designs

of different colours, they varnished them, gilded them and silvered them.

On Friday the whole house smelled of vanilla and cardamom—the cook had begun baking the Easter cakes. By evening on Mamma's bed a dozen big, tall spongecakes and squat Easter yeast cakes were laid out under a towel.

All that week the weather had been uncertain—at first there were heavy black clouds, with a fall of powdery snow, then the sky cleared, the cold spring light shone out of a bottomless blue sky, then there was a blizzard of wet snow. At night the puddles froze over.

On Saturday the estate was empty—half the people from the house and from the workers' quarters had gone to the church at Kolokoltsovka, a village seven versts away, to attend High Mass.

Mamma felt poorly that day—she had worked too hard all the week. Father said that immediately after supper he would go to bed. Arkady Ivanovich who was waiting all the time for a letter from Samara did not get one and sat in his room with the door locked, gloomy as a raven.

They told Nikita that if he wanted to go to High Mass he must find Artyom and tell him to harness the mare Aphrodite to the gig: the mare had been shod on all four feet. He would have to leave before dark and put up with an old friend of Vasily Nikitievich's who kept a grocer's shop in Kolokoltsovka, Pyotr Petrovich Devyatov. "Incidentally, he has a house full of children and you're always alone, it's bad for you," said Mamma.

At dusk Nikita got into the gig beside big Artyom, who wore a new girdle low down on his ragged homespun coat. "Come on, darling, help us," said Artyom, and old Aphrodite with her drooping neck and heavy hind quarters set off at a trot.

They drove out of the yard, past the blacksmith's shop, and crossed the gully with water up to the step. For some reason Aphrodite kept turning her head and looking back at Artyom.

The blue of the evening was reflected in the puddles that were covered with a thin crust of ice. The horse's hoofs crunched along and the gig rattled. Artyom sat in gloomy silence—he was thinking of his unhappy love for Dunyasha. In the greenish sky, in the faint strip of sunset a single star sparkled like a speck of ice.

PYOTR PETROVICH'S CHILDREN

Right up under the ceiling, a lamp with a turned-down, stinking blue flame hung in an iron hoop. On two cloth-covered feather-beds that lay on the floor and smelled pleasantly of home and boys lay Nikita and the six sons of Pyotr Petrovich—Volodya, Kolya, Lyoshka, Lyonka the Whiner and the two little ones whose names didn't interest Nikita.

The eldest boys were telling stories in a low voice. Lyonka the Whiner was constantly in trouble, had his ear pulled or his head punched so that he would not whine. The little ones were asleep, their noses buried in the feather-bed.

87

Pyotr Petrovich's seventh child was a girl, Anna, the same age as Nikita—freckle-faced, with round eyes like a bird's that bore no trace of a smile and a nose that was dark with freckles; from time to time she appeared noiselessly in the door of the boys' room. Then one of the boys would say to her:

"Anna, keep out, or I'll get up in a minute. . . ."

And Anna would disappear as silently as she had come. It was quiet in the house.

Pyotr Petrovich was a church-warden and had gone off to church at dusk.

Marya Mironovna, his wife, said to the children:

"You just make a noise, and I'll knock your heads off. . . ."

She lay down to rest before the early morning High Mass. The children were ordered not to run about. Lyoshka, a round-faced boy with a forelock and his front teeth missing, was telling a tale.

"Last Easter we rolled eggs and I won two hundred of them. I ate and ate until my belly was like this."

From behind the door Anna had her say, afraid that Nikita might believe Lyoshka:

"That's a whopper. Don't you believe him."

"I'm certainly going to get up. . . ." threatened Lyoshka.

There was silence behind the door.

Volodya, the eldest, a swarthy, curly-headed boy, sat up in bed.

"Tomorrow we'll go to the belfry and ring the bells," he told Nikita. "When I begin to ring the whole belfry trembles. I ring the little bells with my left hand—ding, ding—and with this hand I pull the big bell—boom. The big 'un weighs a hundred thousand poods."

"A whopper," came the whisper from behind the door.

Volodya turned round so quickly that his curls flew round his head.

"Anna! . . . And our papa's awful strong," he said. "Papa can pick up a horse by its forelegs. . . . I can't do that yet, of course, but if you come and see us in the summer we'll go out to the pond. Our pond is six versts long. I can climb up a tree, up to the very top, and dive head first into the water from there."

"And I can stay under water without breathing and can see under water," said Lyoshka. "Last summer we went bathing and I got worms and fleas and beetles—as big as this—in my head."

"A whopper," came the scarcely audible whisper from behind the door.

"Anna, I'll get your pigtail! . . ."

"That girl's just a nuisance," said the annoyed Volodya, "she's always poking her nose in our business and then complains to Mother that we hit her."

There was a sob behind the door. The third boy, Kolya, lying on his side with his head supported on his fist, was all the time staring at Nikita with his kindly but rather sad eyes. His face was long in shape and had a modest look about it; there was a wide space between the base of his nose and his upper lip. When Nikita turned towards him he smiled with his eyes.

"Can you swim?" Nikita asked him.

Kolya's eyes laughed. Volodya said carelessly:

"He's the one that reads all the books. In summer he lives on the roof in a tent—yes, a tent on the roof. He lies and reads. Papa wants to send him to the town school. I'm going to look after the shop. Lyoshka is still small so he can run around for a while. Our trouble is this one, the Whiner," he pulled Lyonka's topknot, "he's such a hateful kid. Papa says he's got worms."

"He's got nothing of the sort, I've got terrible worms," said Lyoshka, "because I eat burdocks and acacia pods and I can eat tadpoles."

"A whopper," came the groan from behind the door again.

"Now you'll get it, Anna," and Lyoshka jumped up and made for the door knocking against the baby, who did not wake up but whimpered in his sleep. It sounded as though leaves were being blown down the corridor—of course there was not a trace of Anna, only the sound of a door closing in the distance. As Lyoshka came back he said, "She's run to Mother. Never mind, she won't get away from me: I'll stuff her head full of burrs.'

"Leave her alone, Lyoshka," said Kolya. "What do you keep after her for?"

Lyoshka, Volodya and even Lyonka the Whiner pounded on him:

"We don't keep after her! She hangs on to us. If you go a thousand versts away and look round you'll see her trotting along behind.... There's nothing suits her—we don't tell the truth, do what we're told not to...."

And Lyoshka said:

"Once I sat amongst the reeds in the water all day long so as not to see her and the leeches ate me up."

And Volodya said:

"When we sat down to dinner she immediately told Mother— 'Mamma, Volodya has caught a mouse, he's got it in his pocket.' And for all she knows that mouse may be the dearest thing in the world to me."

And Lyonka the Whiner said:

"She's always standing there looking at you until you want to cry."

As they complained to Nikita about Anna the boys quite forgot that they had been ordered to lie there quietly and not to talk before mass. Suddenly they heard the deep, threatening voice of Marya Mironovna calling from the distance:

"A thousand times I have to tell you...."

The boys stopped talking immediately. Then whispering and pushing each other they began to pull on their boots and don their sheepskin coats; they wound scarves round their necks and ran out into the street.

Marya Mironovna came out in a new plush coat and a shawl decorated with roses. Anna, wrapped up in a big shawl, was holding her mother's hand.

It was a starry night. There was a smell of earth and frost in the air. People were walking along the line of dark cabins in silence, the ice of the puddles, in which the stars were reflected, crunching under their feet—men, women and children on their way to church. The golden dome of the church on the market square could be seen in the distance reaching up into the high heavens. Below the dome oil wicks in saucers arranged in three tiers were burning. A light breeze touched the flames gently.

FIRMNESS OF SPIRIT

After mass they returned home to the festive board where there were red paper roses on the pyramids of sweet cheese, on the Easter cakes and even pinned to the wall. A canary in a cage hanging by the window was twittering—she was worried by the light of the lamp. Pyotr Petrovich, in a long, black frock-coat, laughing into his Tatar moustaches—such was his habit—poured out little glasses of cherry liqueur for everybody. The children began shelling eggs and licking their spoons. Marya Mironovna was so tired that she sat down in her shawl—she was too tired even to eat, she could do nothing but wait until the gang, as she called the children, had settled down.

Nikita had scarcely lain down on the bed under the blue light of the lamp and covered himself with his sheepskin coat before his ears were filled by the singing of thin, chilly voices, "Christ is arisen from the dead, by His death He has conquered death...." And again he saw the white plank walls, the light of countless candles before the gold-leaf frames of the icons; and through the bluish clouds of insense up above him, right under the star-spangled blue of the church dome, he saw a dove with outstretched wings. Outside the grilled window it was night, voices sang, there was a smell of sheepskins, of fresh red bunting—the light of the candles was reflected in thousands of eyes, the western doors opened and the standard-bearers came in, bending down as they entered the door. Everything bad that had been done in the course of the year was forgiven on that night. Anna, with her freckled nose and two blue bows over the ears, stretched over to kiss her brothers....

The morning of the next day was grey and warm. The glad tidings were rung out by all the bells. Nikita and the children of Pyotr Petrovich, even the smallest, went to the barns of the commune on the common. Colours were bright and the place was noisy from the big crowds there. The boys were playing tip-cat, knuckle-bones and picka-back. Girls dressed in brightly coloured shawls and in new, billowing cotton dresses sat on logs by the granary walls. Every one of them held a handkerchief filled with sunflower seeds, raisins and eggs. They nibbled the seeds, looking at the passers-by and laughing merrily.

Young Petka, the elder's son, lolled on the logs at the end, his legs clad in Sunday boots stuck out in front of him, running his fingers over the keys of an accordion; he did not look at anybody but suddenly burst out with a gay village melody.

A circle of lads stood at the other wall playing pitch and toss, each of them with a pile of copper coins in his fist. The one whose turn it was to toss would throw down a five-kopek piece, dig his heel into the ground, put the toe of his boot against a five-kopek piece, kick it up and then toss it into the air shouting, "Heads or tails?"

Sitting on the ground near by, where the buttercups were already peeping through last year's grass, the girls were playing at "find the eggs": a pile of chaff would be divided into two, a couple of eggs hidden in one half and the opponent had to guess which half they were in.

Nikita went up to the group playing "find the eggs," took an egg out of his pocket but immediately heard behind him the voice of Anna, who had come up suddenly, he knew not whence.

"Listen, don't you play with them, they'll cheat you, they'll take all your eggs."

Anna looked at Nikita with her round laughterless eyes and sniffed with her freckled nose. Nikita then went to the boys who were playing knuckle-bones but Anna again appeared from nowhere and whispered out of the corner of her mouth:

"Don't play with them, they're going to cheat you, I heard them."

Wherever Nikita went Anna flew after him like a leaf in the wind and whispered in his ear. Nikita did not know why she kept doing it. He felt very uncomfortable and ashamed, he could see that the boys were beginning to laugh and to stare at him.

"Plays with girls!" one of them shouted.

Nikita went to the cold, blue pond. Dirty melting snow still lay under the steep bank. In the distance the crows were whirling and screaming over the bare trees in the grove. . . .

"Listen," Anna again whispered behind him, "I know where a suslik lives, d'you want to come and look at it?"

Nikita shook his head angrily without turning round.

"Honest, may my eyes burst, I'm not fooling you. Why don't you want to look at the suslik?" she whispered.

"I'm not going."

"All right. D'you want to pick buttercups and rub our eyes with them so that we won't be able to see anything?"

"No, I don't."

"So you don't want to play with me?"

Anna pursed her lips, looked into the pond, at the rippled surface; the wind blew her tightly woven plait to one side, the tip of her freckled nose turned red, her eyes filled with tears and she blinked. Then Nikita realized what was the matter: Anna had been running after him all morning because she felt the same way about him as he did about Lilya.

Nikita walked away swiftly to the edge of the steep bank. If Anna had come after him again he would have jumped into the water, so uncomfortable and ashamed did he feel. He could not exchange those strange words, those meaning glances and smiles with anybody except Lilya. To have done so with any other girl would have been shameless treachery.

"The boys have told you to keep away from me," said Anna, "I'll tell Mummy about all of you.... I'll play by myself.... A lot I need you.... And I know where there's something.... Something interesting...."

Nikita did not turn round, he could hear Anna muttering but he ignored her. His heart was hardened.

SPRING

You could no longer look up at the sun, it already poured its blinding rays down from the heavens. The clouds in the deep blue sky looked like heaps of snow. The spring breezes carried with them odours of fresh grass and birds' nests.

The big buds on the fragrant poplars in front of the house were bursting, chickens clucked in the sunshine. In the garden, green blades of grass peeped through the layer of rotting leaves; the whole field was covered with little white and yellow stars. The number of birds in the garden increased day by day. Blackbirds darted about amongst the tree trunks—they moved on their feet with great agility. Orioles made their nests in the lime-trees—these are big green birds with yellow down that gleams like gold under their wings—and they were fussing about and chirping with their melodious voices.

As soon as the sun came up the starlings on the roofs and in the bird-cotes awoke and added their various voices to the chorus, imitating now nightingales, now larks and then some sort of African birds that they had heard during their winter abroad—scoffing and screaming in horribly unmusical voices. A woodpecker made a patch of grey as he flew through the transparent birches, alighted on a trunk, looked around him and raised his red crest.

On a sunny Sunday morning the cuckoo added his note from the still dew-laden trees by the pond: his sad, lonely and tender voice gave its blessing to every living thing in the garden, beginning with the worms.

"Live, love and laugh, cuckoo! I am living alone, not bothering anyone, cuckoo!..."

The whole garden listened to the cuckoo in silence. The ladybirds, the birds, the eternally astonished frogs squatting on their bellies in the roads and on the balcony steps, were all trying to guess their fate. The cuckoo finished his song and the garden noises took on a jollier air—the leaves began to rustle.

One day Nikita was sitting on the edge of a roadside ditch with his chin in his hands, watching a drove of horses in the level green pasture on the bank of the upper pond. Stately geldings, their tails swishing, lowered their heads and tore at the short grass: mares turned their heads to see whether their foals were following them; the foals on their thin legs with bulbous knees frisked around their dams as though afraid to go too far away; from time to time

95

they nuzzled under their mothers' bellies, took their fill of milk, their tails held high—it was good to get a drink of milk on that spring day.

The three-year-old mares left the herd and dashed round the field, whinnying, kicking and bucking and tossing their heads; one of them began rolling on the grass, another bared her teeth, whinnied and tried to bite her.

Vasily Nikitievich, in a linen coat, drove a drozhky down the road past the dam. His beard was blown to one side, his eyes were screwed up merrily and there was a speck of mud on his cheek. When he saw Nikita he reined in his horse.

"Which horse in the drove do you like best?"

"What for?"

"Without any 'what fors.' "

Nikita screwed his eyes up like his father and pointed to a dark roan gelding called Klopik; he had had his eye on the horse for a long time mostly because it had a good, mild and unusually kindly head.

"That one."

"Excellent. You can go on liking it."

Vasily Nikitievich screwed one eye up tight, smacked his lips, shook the reins and the powerful stallion pulled the drozhky easily along the smooth road. Nikita looked after his departing father: no, he thought, he hadn't been asked for nothing.

RAISING THE FLAG

The sparrows awoke Nikita. He listened and heard the sweet voice, like a whistle blown under water, of an oriole. The window was open, there was a smell of grass and freshness in the room, and the sun's rays were broken by the wet foliage. A breeze was blowing and drops of dew fell on the window-sill. The voice of Arkady Ivanovich came to him from the garden:

"Hi, Admiral, show a leg!"

"I'm getting up!" shouted Nikita but he lay in bed for another minute; it was a wonderful thing when you woke up to hear the voice of the oriole and look out of the window at the wet foliage.

It was Nikita's birthday, the 11th of May, and it was to be celebrated by raising the flag on the pond. Nikita unhurriedly—he did not want the time to pass too rapidly—put on a new shirt, flowered on a blue background, and new breeches that were so strong that he could hang on to any branch of a tree and they would not tear. Satisfied with himself he brushed his teeth.

A big bunch of lilies of the valley stood on the snow-white table-cloth in the dining-room and the whole place was filled with their perfume. Mamma pulled Nikita towards her and, forgetting his rank of admiral, stood for a long time stroking his face and kissing him as though she had not seen him for a year. His father stroked his beard, rolled his eyes and made his report:

"I have the honour to inform Your Excellency that according to the information provided by the Georgian calendar and in conformity with the computations made by the world's astronomers, you reach the age of ten this day for which accomplishment I present you with this penknife containing twelve blades, a fine thing for naval work and to lose."

After breakfast they went down to the pond. Vasily Nikitievich, puffing out his cheeks importantly, whistled a naval march.

Mamma laughed loudly at him—she lifted her skirts so that the hem would not get wet from the dew on the grass. Behind them walked Arkady Ivanovich with the oars and a boat-hook over his shoulder. Beside the bathhouse on the bank of the huge serpentine pond a flag-staff with a ball on top had been erected. The boat stood by the bank, its red and green lines reflected in the water. The population of the pond—the water-beetles, larvae and tiny tadpoles—swam about under the boat's lee. Spiders with cushions on their feet ran along the surface of the water. The rooks looked down at them from their nests in the willows.

Vasily Nikitievich fastened the admiral's personal pennant to the halyard—the device was a red frog standing on its hind legs on a field of green. Puffing out his cheeks he began hauling on the halyard, the pennant ran up the mast and broke at the top. The rooks flew up from their nests in the willows, screaming in alarm.

Nikita got into the boat and took his place at the tiller. Arkady Ivanovich took the oars. The boat settled deeper into the water, swayed and moved off from the bank gliding over the mirror-like surface of the pond which reflected the willows, the green shade beneath them, the birds and the clouds. The boat was floating between earth and sky. A cloud of gnats gathered over Nikita's head— they swarmed together and followed the boat.

"Full speed ahead, full speed!" shouted Vasily Nikitievich from the bank.

Mamma waved her hand and laughed. Arkady Ivanovich lay on

his oars and out of the low green reeds came two quacking ducks, half swimming, half flying in their terror.

"Board her, Admiral of the Frogs! Hurr-a-a-ah!" shouted Vasily Nikitievich.

ZHELTUKHIN *

Zheltukhin was sitting on a tuft of grass in the sun in the corner between the porch and the wall of the house; with fear in his heart he watched the approaching Nikita.

Zheltukhin's head was resting on his back, his beak with the yellow strip running right down it lay on his fat crop. All Zheltukhin's feathers were ruffled, his legs were drawn up under his belly. When Nikita bent over him he opened his beak to frighten the boy. Nikita held him between his two hands. It was a starling, still grey in colour, that had apparently tried to fly away from its nest but its unskilled wings would not support it and it had fallen to the ground and taken refuge in the corner on dandelion leaves pressed close to the earth.

Zheltukhin's heart beat in despair. "Before I can let out a gasp," he thought, "he'll eat me." He knew very well, of course, how to eat worms, flies and caterpillars.

The boy lifted him to his mouth. Zheltukhin's eyes were covered with a film, his heart jumped under his feathers. Nikita, however, only blew on his head and took him into the house: that meant that he was not hungry and would eat Zheltukhin later on.

When Alexandra Leontievna saw the starling she picked him up like Nikita did and blew on his head as he lay on her hand.

"He's so small, the poor little thing," she said. "Such a yellow beak, Zheltukhin."

* The name Zheltukhin comes from the Russian word "zholty" meaning *yellow.—Tr.*

They placed the starling on the sill of a window that opened into the garden and was protected by gauze. The inside of the window was also lined with gauze halfway up. Zheltukhin immediately cringed in the corner striving to show that he would not sell his life cheaply.

Outside, beyond the white gauze, the leaves rustled, the despised sparrows—the thieves and scoundrels—squabbled in the bushes. On the other side, also from behind the gauze, Nikita was looking at him and his eyes were big, they moved, were incomprehensible and enchanting. "I'm lost, I'm lost," thought Zheltukhin.

Still Nikita did not eat him right up to the evening, all he did was drop flies and worms over the gauze. "Fattening me up," thought Zheltukhin and squinted at the red blindworm that was wriggling like a snake in front of his nose. "I won't eat it, it isn't a real worm, it's a trick."

The sun sank below the trees. The grey, sleepy light pulled at his eyes but still Zheltukhin clung tightly to the window-sill with his claws. There was no longer anything to be seen. The birds in the garden grew silent. There was a sweet, somnambulant odour of dampness and grass. His head sank deeper and deeper into his feathers. Ruffling his feathers in anger—in case of emergency—Zheltukhin lurched forward, then backward on to his tail and fell asleep.

The sparrows woke him up—they were creating a disturbance, fighting on the branches of a lilac-tree. Wet leaves hung down in the greyish light. Sweetly and merrily, to the accompaniment of clucking, a starling sang in the distance. "I can't stand it, I'm so hungry that I feel sick," thought Zheltukhin and saw the worm that had crept halfway into a crack in the window-sill, jumped on it, pulled it out by its tail and swallowed it. "Not bad, a tasty worm," he thought.

The light changed to blue. The birds began to sing. A bright, warm ray of sunshine fell on Zheltukhin through the leaves of the trees.

"Well, we're still alive," thought Zheltukhin, hopped along, snapped up a fly and swallowed it.

At that moment there came the sound of footsteps, Nikita came to the window and pushed his huge hand behind the gauze: he opened his fingers and scattered flies and worms on the window-sill. Zheltukhin cringed back into his corner in terror, spread his wings, looked at the hand but it hovered over his head and then disappeared behind the gauze; again those strange, absorbing, opalescent eyes stared at Zheltukhin.

When Nikita had gone, Zheltukhin preened his feathers and began to think: "So he didn't eat me although he could have. So he doesn't eat birds. Then there's nothing to be afraid of."

Zheltukhin ate his fill, preened his feathers with his bill, hopped along the window-sill, looked out at the sparrows, saw an old one with tattered head feathers and began teasing him, turning his head back and forth and whistling: "Fuyoot, chillik-chillik, fuyoot." The sparrow grew angry, puffed up his chest and flew at Zheltukhin with open beak—and flew straight into the gauze. "Got what was coming to you," thought Zheltukhin and strutted up and down the window-sill.

Then Nikita came back again, thrust his hand behind the gauze, but this time it was empty and he held it too near the bird. Zheltukhin jumped at it and pecked at a finger with all his strength, jumped back and made ready for battle. But Nikita only opened his mouth and roared, "Ha, ha, ha."

And so the day passed, there was nothing to fear, the food was good if a little monotonous, Zheltukhin could scarcely wait for sundown and slept that night in complete satisfaction.

Next day, after he had had his breakfast, he began to look for a way to escape from behind the gauze. He hopped around the whole window but there was not a single crack anywhere. Then he jumped on to his dish and began to drink—he filled his beak with water, threw back his head and swallowed—a little round ball rolled down his throat.

It was a long day. Nikita brought worms and cleaned the window-sill with a goose feather. Then the bald sparrow quarrelled with a jackdaw who struck him such a blow that he dropped through the leaves like a stone and looked up, all bristling.

For some reason or another a magpie flew right close to the window, trilled a few notes, darted about, wagged his tail and did nothing that had any sense to it.

A robin sang for a long time, sang sweetly about the hot sunlight, about honey in the clover—it made Zheltukhin so sad and there was such a gurgling in his throat, he too wanted to sing, but where could he sing, not in the window, in a cage!...

He again made his tour of the window-sill and saw a fearful animal: it crept along on short soft legs, its belly dragging along the floor. Its head was round, its sparse whiskers stood out stiff, its eyes were green, their narrow pupils gleaming with Satanic evil. Zheltukhin squatted down and did not budge.

Vasily Vasilievich the cat jumped softly, held on to the edge of the window-sill with his claws, looked through the gauze at Zheltukhin and opened his mouth.... Oh Lord, in the mouth ... longer than Zheltukhin's beak ... were fangs!... The cat struck out with his paw and tore the gauze.... Zheltukhin's heart sank, his wings hung down.... Just then, and just in time, Nikita appeared and seized the cat by the loose skin on the back of his neck and hurled him towards the door. Vasily Vasilievich whined angrily and ran away with his tail down.

"There's no animal stronger than Nikita," thought Zheltukhin after this incident and when Nikita came again he let the boy stroke his head although he sat back on his tail in fear.

And so that day ended. The next morning a very happy Zheltukhin went on a tour of inspection around his premises and immediately saw the hole in the gauze that the cat had made. Zheltukhin put his head through the hole, looked round, climbed out, sprang into the stream of light air and, flapping his wings frantically, flew along just above the floor.

When he reached the door he flew up into the other room where he saw four people seated at a round table. They were eating, they took up huge pieces of food and placed them in their mouths. All four of them turned their heads and, motionless, watched Zheltukhin. He knew that he should stop short in the air and turn round, but he could not make that difficult turn in flight, flopped over on to one wing and landed on the table between the jam dish and the sugar bowl. Then he noticed Nikita sitting in front of him. Without thinking Zheltukhin hopped on to the jam dish, from there on to Nikita's shoulder and there he sat with his feathers ruffled and his eyes even half-covered with film.

He remained seated on Nikita's shoulder for a while, then flew up under the ceiling, caught a fly, alighted on the ficus in the corner, cruised round the candelabra, began to feel hungry and flew back to his own window where fresh worms were waiting for him.

Towards evening Nikita brought a little wooden house with a porch, a door and two windows and put it on the window-sill. Zheltukhin liked it—the inside was dark, he hopped in, turned round a couple of times and then went to sleep.

That same night, Vasily Vasilievich, locked in a storeroom as punishment for his attempted crime, had mewed hoarsely and did not even want to catch mice—he just sat at the door and miauled so pitifully that he even felt uncomfortable himself.

The house now contained a third member of the animal kingdom—in addition to the hedgehog and the cat—Zheltukhin. He was very independent, clever and resourceful. He liked to listen to people talking and when they sat down to table he would listen, cock his head on one side and warble in singsong tones, "Sasha!" and would bow. Alexandra Leontievna believed that he was bowing to her. Whenever she saw Zheltukhin she would say to him, "Greetings, greetings, little birdie, full of life and joy." Zheltukhin would immediately hop on to the train of her dress and ride along with a very satisfied air.

And so he lived until autumn; he grew up, acquired big flashing black wings and feathers, learned to speak Russian well and lived almost all day in the garden, always returning to his little house on the window-sill at dusk.

In August wild starlings enticed him into their flock, taught him to fly properly and when the leaves in the garden began to fall he flew off at break of day across the sea to Africa with the birds of passage.

KLOPIK

The spring work in the fields was over, the orchard had been dug up and watered and now there was nothing left to do until St. Peter's day when the mowing would begin. The draught-horses were driven out with the herds into the meadows beyond the pond where there was luscious grass; in the mornings there was bluish mist over the fields and the huge black poplars, each standing aloof from the others, seemed to be growing out of the opaque air and to be hanging over the earth.

Mishka Koryashonok remained with the herd to look after the horses. He rode in a high Cossack saddle, his bare feet in the stirrups and his elbows flapping.

Galloping across the green fields after a young mare that had strayed from the herd he cracked his whip like a pistol-shot and shouted at her to get back. Then he would slip down from the unbridled horse that immediately began tearing at the grass with its dangling bit clanking and would either sit on the mound above the ditch and whittle sticks or would roll up his trousers, walk into the pond and pull the bulbs and roots of the reeds out of the warm water: the roots were long and black, like snakes. The bulbs had a sourish taste but the roots were floury and sweet although they made your tummy ache if you ate too many of them.

Nikita spent the whole day with Mishka in the field beyond the pond and learned to ride a horse.

It was not difficult to get into the saddle: the old flea-bitten Grey stood quiet enough, only occasionally scratching its belly with its hind-leg to brush away the horse-flies. But when he had mounted, taken the reins and set the Grey at a trot Nikita began to fall first to one side and then to the other. When the Grey trotted about thirty paces and would then stop suddenly and put its head down to eat grass, Nikita would grasp the pommel of the saddle with all his strength and some-times would even slide over the horse's neck and land at her feet; the old horse treated all this with absolute indifference.

Said Mishka:

"Don't be scared, falling doesn't hurt, only pull in your neck and don't, for God's sake, try to grab the ground with your hands, curl up in a ball. I'll show you how to do it without saddle or bridle, just jump on and fly away."

Mishka ran towards a group of three-year-olds that had never been backed and holding out his hand began to call them:

"Feed, feed, feed...."

Star, a spoiled, thin-legged, dapple-grey mare, came towards him, her ears flat and her velvet lips hunting for grain. Mishka began to scratch her neck. Star tossed her fine head, the scratching was pleasant and, in order to please Mishka, she took his shoulder in her teeth.

Mishka stroked her, ran his hand along her satin back—Star stepped back alarmed—seized her by the withers and sprang on to her back. Astonished and angry Star sprang to one side, tossed her head, bucked, squatted on her hind-legs, reared and then raced past the herd at a stretch gallop.

Mishka sat glued to her back. Suddenly she stopped dead in her tracks and backed, Mishka rolled over in a ball on the grass. He limped as he walked back to Nikita rubbing the blood away from his grazed cheek.

"Straight into the twigs that blasted mare threw me," he said, "but you can't do it, you're too fat."

"I'll break my neck but I'll learn to ride better than Mishka," thought Nikita.

He spoke about Star at the dinner-table which worried Mamma rather a lot.

"Listen," she said, "I ask you not even to go near the unbroken horses," and she looked beseechingly at Vasily Nikitievich. "Vasya, at least you can support me.... He'll end up by breaking his arms and legs...."

"Excellent," answered Vasily Nikitievich, "forbid him to ride and forbid him to walk while you're about it, he may fall and hurt his nose—put him in a jar, pack him in cotton-wool and send him away to a museum."

"It's what I expected," said Mamma, "I knew there wouldn't be a moment's peace for me this summer...."

"Sasha, you must understand that the boy's ten years old."

"It's all the same...."

"Pardon me, please, I don't want him to grow up into a molly-coddle."

"All right, but that doesn't mean you can make him a present of Klopik immediately."

"In the first place, an infant in arms could ride Klopik."

"He's been shod."

"I have ordered him to be unshod."

"In that case do whatever you want, ride wild horses, break your necks," Mamma's eyes filled with tears, she got up quickly from the table and went into the bedroom.

Vasily Nikitievich rapidly stroked his beard into two parts, threw down his napkin and went to Mamma. Arkady Ivanovich, who had sat there all the time as though the conversation had nothing to do with him, looked at Nikita, adjusted his glasses, and said in a whisper:

"Things aren't going too well with you, brother."

"Arkady Ivanovich, tell Mamma that I won't fall, on my honour, I won't. . . ."

"Patience, endurance and firmness of character," Arkady Ivanovich adroitly caught a fly that was persistently trying to settle on his nose, "are three qualities that are also needed if you want to ride well."

There was a loud conversation going on in the bedroom all the time. Said Father's voice: "At his age boys are quite independent." "Where are they independent?" asked Mamma's despairing voice. "In America they're independent." "That's not true." "I tell you that in America ten-year-old boys are as independent as I am." "My God, but we're not in America. . . ."

The talk about independence lasted a whole week. Mamma was already surrendering and looked sadly at Nikita, as though he were certain to be broken up but she hoped that he might manage to save his head.

During the same week Nikita was persistently taking riding-lessons in the field by the pond—Mishka praised him and taught him a rough-rider's trick—to take a running jump and vault on to the horse over its croup, like playing leap-frog.

"She can't buck you off, she can't do it in time, by the time she bucks you're already on her withers."

At long last, after breakfast on the balcony where the Indian cresses climbing up strings cast moving shadows on the table-cloth, plates and faces, Mamma called Nikita over, made him stand in front of her and said in a sad voice:

"You're ten years old, you know, and you must be independent, at your age other boys are quite, quite—" her voice shook and she frowned slightly towards Father. "In short, Papa's right, you are no longer a child." Vasily Nikitievich dropped his eyes and drummed on the edge of the table with his fingers. "Tomorrow we are going to visit Chembulatova and you may ride over on Klopik.... Only I ask you, I beseech you—"

"Mamma, on my word of honour nothing will happen to me," and Nikita kissed Mamma's eyes, cheeks, chin and hands that smelled of berries.

The next day, after an early dinner, Vasily Nikitievich told Nikita to take his saddle—an English grey chamois saddle presented to him at Christmas—and told him as they walked across the grass to the stables:

"You must learn to groom a horse, to saddle it and to rub it down after a ride. The horse must be properly curried, he must be clean. If he is, you're a good cavalryman."

In the wide-open coach-house a three-horse team was being harnessed to a carriage. Sergei Ivanovich the coachman, in his sleeveless jacket, crimson shirt but an ordinary cap—he only donned his feathered hat when he was ready to mount the box—was adjusting the traces and cursing Artyom, who was helping him.

"What are you putting the strap under his chest for, ignoramus! This is a carriage harness. Don't touch the throatlash. You couldn't harness a cat to a basket."

"I have never had a horse."

"The girls won't have you because you're an ignoramus. Give me the new reins."

Byron, the shaft-horse, standing harnessed in the wide-open doors, champed its bit, pawed the board floor and playfully took Sergei Ivanovich's shoulder between his teeth as the latter arranged the horse's forelock under the browband. The coach-house smelled of leather, healthy horse sweat and pigeons. When the horses were harnessed Sergei Ivanovich turned to Nikita with a faint smile.

"D'you want to saddle up yourself?"

Klopik was brought from the stables. Nikita looked at him in excitement.

Klopik was a roan, well-groomed, short, sturdy gelding with white stockings, a thick, dark tail and mane. He had a big forelock that covered his eyes and he tossed his head looking merrily from under the hair. There was a long black line down his back.

"A fine horse," said Sergei Ivanovich as he fetched a pail of water. Klopik drank and then lifted his head with the water trickling down from his grey lips.

Nikita took the headstall and, as he had been taught, put the bit in the horse's mouth from one side and fastened the throatlash. Klopik took the steel between his teeth. Nikita put the saddle blanket in place, covered it with a grey horse-cloth with initials in the corner, threw the saddle over the horse's back and began tightening the girth—it was no easy task for him.

"He blows out his belly," said Sergei Ivanovich. "The cunning beast blows out his belly," and he slapped Klopik's belly with his hand; the gelding blew the air out of his mouth and Nikita pulled the girth up tight.

Vasily Nikitievich came up and began to give instructions.

"Take the reins in the left hand, approach the horse from the front, from the near shoulder. Mount. Take up the slack till he feels the bit. Don't dangle your feet in the stirrups, don't turn your toes down."

Nikita mounted, found the elusive off stirrup with a trembling leg, touched the horse with his heels and away went Klopik at a trot towards the stables.

Vasily Nikitievich shouted:

"Halt! Stop! Use your off rein, clumsy."

Klopik stopped in the shade of the stables. Nikita was hot from shame, dismounted, took the horse by the bridle and led him out, whispering all the time to the sly gelding:

"Swine, you're a real swine, you poor idiot!..."

Klopik jauntily tossed his forelock. Sergei Ivanovich came up to them.

"Mount and I'll lead him out. He's a cunning young beast. He doesn't want to work, wants to stand in the shade."

At last Klopik was under control and Nikita cantered him along past the cattle sheds.

Sergei Ivanovich donned his feathered hat, his white, floured gloves, mounted the box and shouted sternly:

"Let 'em go!"

Artyom, who was holding Byron by the bridle, jumped away and the carriage, rattling over the boards, flew out of the coach-house flashing copper and varnish, fresh turves flying from under the heels of the trace-horses, the matched harness bells tinkling; the carriage described a half-circle round the yard and halted outside the house.

Alexandra Leontievna, wearing a white dress, came down from the porch, opened a white parasol; she looked in alarm at Nikita who was prancing away in the distance. Father seated Mamma in the carriage and then climbed in himself.

"Drive away!"

Sergei Ivanovich lifted the reins. The splendid dark-bay horses, fretting at their tight bits, pulled the carriage away easily, their hoofs rattled over the boardwalk and the trace-horses fell into a gallop; the team got into its stride. Byron realized that this was all a joke and flattened his ears. Mamma kept glancing round. Nikita had slackened his reins, was bending low over the horse's neck and racing hell for leather after the carriage.

He wanted to race madly past but Klopik had a different idea—he thought it was all a waste of time and when he drew level with the carriage he turned on to the road, dropped into a trot just behind the wheels in a cloud of dust. Nothing could check him or turn him off the road: he thought it was all unnecessary, if one had to ride one should ride on the road and all argument was useless.

Mamma looked round. Nikita was jerking, his lips were pressed together and he was looking intently between the horse's ears. The dust made him feel sick and the horse's trot upset his stomach.

"D'you want to get into the carriage?"

Nikita stubbornly shook his head. Father, smiling, turned to Sergei Ivanovich.

"Let them go all out!"

Byron pricked up his ears, his iron legs began to work with a will and the trace-horses spread out on to the grass verge. Klopik broke into a gallop but the carriage gradually drew away from him and he grew angry and galloped with all his might, making a great effort.

The sickening sensation of the jog-trot passed away and Nikita sat easily and firmly in his saddle, the wind whistling in his ears; at the side of the road there were waves of green corn and the sweet voices of larks, unseen in the sunlight, rang out. ... It was almost as good as in Fenimore Cooper.

The carriage horses slowed down to a walk. Nikita overtook the carriage and, panting, looked happily at his father.

"All right, Nikita?"

"Marvellous. ... Klopik's a wonderful horse."

111

IN THE SWIMMING-POOL

Early one morning Vasily Nikitievich, Arkady Ivanovich and Nikita walked in single file along a path through grass that was grey with the dew; they were going to the pond to bathe.

The early morning mist still filled the thickets in the garden. Butterflies hovered like tiny leaves over the nectar-bearing yellow cowslips and the white clover in the glade where a worried bee was buzzing around. A wild dove cooed in the thicket—he closed his eyes, puffed out his chest and cooed, sweetly and sadly, that it would always be like this, it would pass but it would begin all over again.

Vasily Nikitievich crossed the footbridge whose long boards slapped on the water and entered the dressing-room where he undressed on a bench that stood in the shadow; he slapped his white hairy chest, his smooth sides, squinted at the sparkling water and said:

"Fine, excellent!"

His sun-burned face and flashing beard seemed to have been as an afterthought to his white body. Father had a particularly fine fragrance of health about him. Whenever a fly alighted on his leg or his shoulder he would slap it loudly with his open hand leaving a pink mark on his skin. When he had cooled off, Father took a piece of toilet soap, a very light kind that did not sink in the water, and walked carefully down the slippery, moss-covered steps into the bathing-pool—the water came up to his chest—and began vigorously soaping his head and beard snorting and muttering:

"Fine, excellent."

Over the top of the bathing-pool there was a swarm of midges in the bluish sunlight. A dragonfly floated past, looked in alarm with its bulging green eyes at Vasily Nikitievich's lathered head and flew off sideways. Arkady Ivanovich, in the meantime, was hurriedly and bashfully undressing; he curled up his long toes, opened the outer door of the dressing-room and looked out to make sure that nobody could see him from the bank and said in a deep bass, "Ugh, fine," and plunged flat on his belly in the pond. The water splashed up in all directions, the scared rooks flew up from the willows, and he swam with big, long strokes, his body with its reddish hair wriggling under the blue water.

When he reached the middle of the pond Arkady Ivanovich began turning somersaults, he dived and reappeared, grunting like a water monster, "Ugh, br-r-r-r."

Nikita sat curled up on the resinous bench and waited until his father finished washing. Vasily Nikitievich placed the soap on the steps, stuck his fingers in his ears and ducked three times—the wet hair stuck to his head, his beard hung down like a goat's and in general he had the appearance of an unfortunate being: in fact, they had a name for this—it was called "playing at Unfortunate Vasya."

"Now let's have a swim," he said, and went out of the door and plunged heavily into the water. He swam like a frog, slowly moving his arms and legs in the clear water.

Nikita plunged head first into the water and, overtaking his father, swam beside him, waiting for praise from him; that summer Nikita had learned to swim well by accompanying the boys who bathed in the Chagry River—he could swim on his side and his back, could tread water and turn a somersault under water.

"Let's duck Arkady," said Father in a whisper.

They parted and swam from two directions towards Arkady Ivanovich who was so shortsighted that he could not see anything even near him. With long strokes they swam up close and jumped on him. Arkady Ivanovich got mad at them, began darting this way and that, lifted himself out of the water up to his waist and then dived under; they tried to catch him by the feet for he hated being tickled more than anything else. It was not very easy to catch him, however, he nearly always escaped and when Vasily Nikitievich and Nikita returned to the dressing-room he was already sitting on the bench in his underclothes and glasses.

"You must learn to swim, gentlemen," he said with a chuckle of annoyance.

When they returned from these excursions they usually met Alexandra Leontievna in a white mob-cap and a fluffy dressing-gown.

"Breakfast is laid under the lime-trees in the garden," said Mamma, screwing up her eyes in the sunlight and smiling. "You start, don't wait for me, the rolls will get cold."

THE BAROMETER NEEDLE

For several days Vasily Nikitievich has been tapping the barometer with his thumb-nail and cursing in a whisper: the needle showed "Dry. Very Dry." For a fortnight not a drop of rain had fallen and it was time for the grain to ripen. The earth was cracking, the sky looked washed-out in the heat and in the distance, on the horizon there was a dark haze that looked like the dust raised by a herd of cattle. The meadows burned up, the leaves on the trees drooped and began to curl and no matter how often Vasily Nikitievich tapped the barometer the needle still indicated: "Dry. Very Dry."

When they met at table the family did not joke as was their wont; Father and Mother went about with a worried look on their faces; Arkady Ivanovich was also silent, he stared at his plate and from time to time adjusted his glasses, trying to cover up a surreptitious sigh by these subterfuges. He, however, had his own reasons: Vassa Nilovna, the city schoolmistress, who had promised to come to Sosnov-ka on a visit, had written that she was "chained to the bed of her sick mother" and did not expect to see Arkady Ivanovich before autumn in Samara.

That is just how Nikita imagined that Vassa Nilovna: a tall, downcast woman in a grey blouse with a watch on a silk cord and one leg fastened to the bed by a chain. In those days that were stifling and gloomy from the heat haze, the city schoolmistress sitting beside an iron bed against a bare wall presented a particularly dismal picture.

At lunch Vasily Nikitievich sat rhythmically tapping the edge of his plate.

"If it doesn't rain tomorrow there'll be no harvest," he said.

Mamma immediately lowered her head. They could hear a fly buzzing madly in the big window, in the top part where there were double semicircular panes that were never cleaned and had cobwebs in between them. The French windows leading to the balcony were closed to keep out the heat from the garden.

"Surely there won't be another famine year," said Mamma. "Oh, my God, how awful!"

"That's how things stand: sit still and await the sentence." Father walked over to the window and glanced up at the sky, his hands thrust into the pockets of his tussore silk trousers. "Another day of this hellish heat and we'll have a hungry winter, typhus, cattle dying off, children dying.... It's beyond all reason."

They finished lunch in silence. Father went to bed. Mother had to go to the kitchen to check the linen. Arkady Ivanovich, in order to put himself into an even worse mood, went out for a walk in the burning steppe.

In the evil silence that filled the rooms in the afternoon nothing could be heard but the buzzing of the flies; everything seemed damped by a layer of dust. Nikita did not know what to do with himself. He went on to the porch. In the hazy but blinding white light of the sun the yard was empty and silent—everything was asleep, dead. His head rang from the silence and the heat.

Nikita went into the garden but there was no life there, either. A sleepy bee buzzed. The dusty leaves hung motionless as though made of tin. The boat lay still deep in the muddy pond, rooks had covered its sides with white spots.

Nikita went back home and lay down on a small sofa that smelled of mice. In the middle of the room stood a clothless dining-table with a large number of disgusting thin legs. There was nothing in the world more boring than that table. Far away in the kitchen the cook was singing softly—she was most probably cleaning the knives with brick-dust and was howling, howling in a low voice from deadly boredom.

And suddenly on the sill of a half-open window Zheltukhin appeared, his bill half open because of the heat. When he regained his breath he flew across the room and alighted on Nikita's shoulder. Turning his head he looked Nikita in the eyes, then pecked at his temple where the boy had a black birth-mark that looked like a grain of millet, felt it and then looked into his eyes again.

"Leave me alone, please, and go away," Nikita said to him; he got up lazily and filled the starling's saucer with water.

Zheltukhin drank his fill, jumped into the saucer, took a dip, splashed all the water out of the saucer, and then began to look round cheerfully for a place where he could shake and preen himself; he alighted on the ledge of the wooden barometer.

"Fuweet," said Zheltukhin in a tender voice. "Fuweet, sto-r-r-m."

"What d'you say?" asked Nikita going over to the barometer.

Zheltukhin bowed as he sat there on the ledge, lowered his wings and muttered something in bird language and something else in Russian. And then Nikita noticed that the blue needle of the barometer had moved far away from the golden needle and was hesitating between "Variable" and "Storm."

Nikita drummed on the glass with his fingers and the needle moved farther towards the "Storm" division. Nikita ran to the library where his father was sleeping. He knocked at the door and a dull, sleepy voice called out:

"Who is it? What's the matter?"

"Papa, come and look at the barometer...."

"Don't bother me, Nikita, I'm sleeping."

"But come and look what's happening to the barometer, Papa...."

It was very quiet in the library and apparently Father was unable to wake up. At last his bare feet shuffled across the floor, the key turned in the lock and a tousled beard looked out of the crack of the door.

"Why did you wake me up? What's the matter?"

"The barometer is pointing to 'Storm.'"

"I don't believe you," said Father in a scared whisper and ran into the drawing-room; he immediately shouted for the whole house to hear: "Sasha, Sasha, a storm! Hurrah! We're saved!"

The oppression and the heat grew worse. The birds grew silent, the dazed flies swarmed on the windows. Towards evening the low sun disappeared into the burning haze. Twilight came on very fast. It was pitch-dark, not a single star shining. The barometer was set firm at "Storm." The whole family had gathered round the centipede table. They spoke in whispers, glancing towards the open balcony doors that led into the invisible garden.

In the deadly silence the first motion came from the willows on the pond whose rustling was accompanied by the cries of the alarmed rooks. Father went out on to the dark balcony. The noises grew louder and more triumphant, until at last a strong gust of wind flattened the acacia by the balcony carrying the smells of the fields and several dead leaves into the house; the flame of the opaque lamp-shade flickered and the wind, growing in fury, howled and shrieked in the chimneys and round the corners of the house. Somewhere a window slammed and there was a sound of breaking glass, the tree-trunks groaned as their invisible crowns swayed in the wind. Vasily Nikitievich, his hair dishevelled, returned from the balcony, his mouth was open and his eyes seemed bigger. A blinding whitish-blue flash broke the darkness of the night and the low, wind-bent trees appeared for an instant as black silhouettes. Then darkness again. With a roar the whole heavens descended. On account of the noise they did not hear the raindrops strike and run down the window-panes. The rain was strong, abundant, it poured down in torrents. Mamma stood at the balcony doors, her eyes filled with tears. The smell of dampness, of rot, rain and grass filled the room.

THE NOTE

Nikita slipped out of his saddle, tied Klopik up to a nail in the black and white post outside the post-office in the market-place of the village of Utyovka.

Behind the open barrier sat the tousle-headed, puffy-faced postmaster melting sealing wax over a candle. The table at which he sat was covered with sealing wax and ink-stains and sprinkled with tobacco ash. When he had accumulated sufficient wax on the envelope he seized the stamp in his hairy hand and brought it down on the wax with as much force as if he wanted to crush the skull of the sender. Then he fumbled in the table drawer, pulled out a stamp, stuck out his huge tongue, licked the stamp, stuck it on the envelope, spat disgustedly and only then turned his bloodshot eyes on Nikita.

The postmaster's name was Ivan Ivanovich Landyshev. He was in the habit of reading all the newspapers and magazines and until he had read them from cover to cover would not even think of delivering them. Complaints had been lodged against him in Samara but he did not give up his reading, only grew more bad-tempered. He got drunk six times a year and then people were afraid even to enter the post-office. On such days the postmaster would stick his head out of the window and shout across the whole market-place, "You've eaten away my soul, curse you!"

"Papa sent me for the mail," said Nikita.

The postmaster did not answer him, again began to melt sealing wax, dropped a spot on his hand, jumped up, howled and sat down again.

"How am I supposed to know who

your papa is?" he muttered in a grumpy voice. "Everybody here is a papa, they're all papas. . . ."

"What did you say?"

"That you have a thousand fathers, I say," the postmaster even spat under the table. "Your name, your name, tell me, what's that papa's name?" He threw down the sealing wax and when Nikita answered him, pulled a bundle of letters out of the drawer.

Nikita put the letters in his bag and asked timidly:

"And aren't there any magazines or papers?"

The postmaster began to blow out his cheeks. Nikita did not wait for an answer but ran out of the door.

At the hitching post Klopik was stamping his feet and swishing himself with his tail to get rid of the flies that swarmed on him. Two little boys with flaxen hair, their faces daubed with some red substance, were looking at the horse.

"Mind out of the way," shouted Nikita as he climbed into the saddle.

One of the boys sat down in the dust, the other turned round and ran away. In the window he could see that the postmaster had again taken up his sealing wax.

When Nikita left the village and rode out into the open steppe, hot and golden-yellow from the ripening corn, he allowed Klopik to go at his own pace, opened his bag and looked through the letters.

There was one little letter in a lavender-coloured envelope on which was an inscription in big letters: "For Nikita." The note was written on lace paper. Blinking his eyes in excitement, Nikita read:

"Dear Nikita,

"I haven't forgotten you. I love you very much. We are living at the summer cottage. It is a lovely little cottage. Although Victor does bother me a lot; he won't leave me alone. He has got quite out of hand.

120

He has had his hair cropped off with the machine for the third time and goes about all covered in scratches. I play in the garden alone. We have a swing and even apples, but they aren't ripe yet. Do you remember the magic forest? Come and see us in Samara in the autumn. I haven't lost your ring yet. Good-bye.

"Lilya."

Nikita read that wonderful letter several times over. Suddenly the memory of the glorious days of the Christmas holidays came back to him. The candles were burning. Shadows danced on the walls, the big bow appeared over the penetrating blue eyes of a girl, the paper chains rustled and the moonlight sparkled on the frost-bound windows. The snow-covered roofs, white trees and the fields of snow were flooded with a transparent light.... Lilya again sat at the round table under the lamp, her head rested on her fist.... Magic!...

Nikita stood up in his stirrups and cracked his whip—his action was so sudden that Klopik jumped to one side and broke into a canter. The wind whistled in his ears. An eagle soared high over the steppes, over the ripe grain that in some places had already been cut and over the clayey bank of the river. The peewits screamed plaintively and

forlornly around a saline lake in a hollow. "Run, run, run," thought Nikita. His heart was happy and beating fast. "Blow, blow, wind!... Fly, fly, eagle!... Scream, scream, you peewits, I am happier than you. The wind and I, the wind and I...."

THE FAIR AT PESTRAVKA

Vasily Nikitievich and Mamma had been quarrelling for three days: Father wanted to go to the fair at Pestravka but Mamma was very much opposed to the trip.

"In Pestravka, my friend, they'll manage very well without you."

"Strange," answered Father, taking up a handful of his beard, biting it and shrugging his shoulders, "that's very strange."

"Think it strange if you like, my friend."

"But it is peculiar, more than peculiar, in fact."

"I tell you again," repeated Mamma, "we don't need any new horses: the stable is full of riding-horses, God knows!"

"Will you at last understand that I am going to sell Zaremka, that accursed mare."

"You shouldn't, Zaremka's a good horse."

"You think so!" Father spread his legs and his eyes bulged. "Zaremka bites and bucks."

"No," answered Mamma firmly, "Zaremka does not bite or buck."

"In that case," Father even bowed politely, "here is my ultimatum: either I leave the place or that accursed mare does."

In the end, Mamma, as Nikita had expected, gave way to Father. The quarrel ended in a truce with concessions: they decided to sell the mare and Father promised "not to spend crazy sums of money at the fair."

In order to make good any expenses, Vasily Nikitievich decided to send two cart-loads of apples, windfalls, to Pestravka and to sell them retail.

Nikita asked and obtained permission to go with Mishka Koryasho-nok on the carts.

From the very morning there were hitches. The horses were not ready and Mishka Koryashonok flew away on the trace-horse to the herd that was scarcely visible in the morning haze on the low-lying lands beyond the ponds. Then when Zaremka, a roan mare with white stockings, was brought from the stables and the grooms began to curry her she caught hold of Sergei Ivanovich with her teeth and almost bit into him. Father saw it all from the window and ran to the stables in his night-clothes.

"So she does bite! I told you so, you accursed devils."

Zaremka began pulling back, sitting on her haunches, dragged Sergei Ivanovich around as he held on to her headstall, whinnied, broke away and lowering her head and bucking so that the clumps of earth from her hind-legs flew over the coach-house, she galloped away to the herd. Then it was discovered that Artyom, who was to go with the carts, had disappeared. A search was made and it was discovered that he was in the lock-up for arrears on taxes—Artyom was about five years in arrears and an order had been given that wherever he was to be found he was to be arrested and put in the lock-up until somebody bailed him out.

Vasily Nikitievich sent a mounted messenger to the village elder and Artyom was let out on bail; he came to harness the carts in a merry mood. The carts were ready at last and Zaremka was tied to the rear cart. Nikita and Mishka Koryashonok climbed on to the front cart. Artyom slapped the horse with his reins and the carts moved off.... Sergei Ivanovich played a joke on him. Pointing to the wheel he shouted:

"Look, the linchpin." Artyom got down again, looked at the wheel, but the linchpin was quite all right. He scratched his head, shook it.... At last they got off.

It was a fine journey. There was a slight breeze blowing that smelled of wormwood and wheat straw and tossed the leaves of the burdocks between the fields. From the haystacks, that stood all over the level steppes wherever you looked, a hawk arose and soared slowly across the sky. In the distance arose a blue smoke where food was being cooked in the ploughmen's camp.

They arrived at the camp and found a caravan there. Artyom pulled up the horses and the boys went to a barrel to drink pond water that smelled of the barrel and was full of infusoria. The aged man who cooked for the ploughmen laid his hand on the side of the cart and, shaking his bare head, said:

"Taking apples to sell?" Nikita offered him an apple. "No thanks, lad, I've nothing to bite it with."

As they left the camp they met four herdsmen: tousle-headed ploughmen in sweat-hardened shirts were walking behind oxen dragging ploughs, shares up, and stumbling in the pot-holes. They were on their way back to camp for dinner. Artyom again stopped and spent a long time asking which way to turn off the road to get to Pestravka.

By midday the breeze died down and waves of heat arose in the distance, at the very edge of the steppes. Peering into that trembling blue haze Nikita saw now a floating house, now a tree hanging over the earth, now a ship without its masts. The carts drove on. Grasshoppers chirped. Then there came the regular musical sound of bells across the steppe. Zaremka danced and side-stepped, and then neighed loudly. Artyom turned round and said with a wink:

"That's the master coming!"

Soon a team of three horses dashed past the carts—Byron, his head thrown back, was moving along at a swinging trot with the high-rumped trace-horses snapping at the ground in anger. Father sat in the carriage with his arms akimbo—he was wearing a tussore jacket and his beard was blown out on either side by the wind; glancing round with merry eyes he shouted to Nikita:

"D'you want to come with me?" And the carriage rolled past.

At last the two domes of the white church, the poles over the wells, the tops of occasional willows, wisps of smoke and roofs gradually appeared; beyond the clayey-yellow river, sparkling in the sun, the whole village of Pestravka came into view and in the fields on the far side of the village there were the marquees of the fair and herds of animals making black patches.

The carts went over a rickety bridge just above the level of the water at a trot, passed the church square where a fat priest was playing the fiddle in the corner window of a pink house, turned into the field where the fair booths stood and came to a halt near the place where the potters had their stand.

Nikita stood up in the cart and looked: a Gypsy in a blue caftan with silver buttons that was open on his bare chest and with a black beard that came right up to his eyes was examining the teeth of a sick horse, while a feeble little peasant, the horse's owner, looked at the Gypsy in astonishment. Then there was a cunning old man trying to persuade a scared woman to buy a pot decorated with a grass-leaf design which he was

tapping with his finger-nail. "But I don't want that sort of pot at all," said the woman. "You may search the whole world and not find a pot like that, dearie." A drunken peasant was shouting angrily beside a basket full of eggs: "D'you call those eggs? D'you think they're eggs—they're feeble! In our village of Koldyban we have eggs that are eggs, in Koldyban, I say, the chickens are up to their necks in grain." Girls in pink and yellow blouses and brightly coloured kerchiefs turned towards the marquees where shouting salesmen leaned over their counters and seized passers-by: "Come to us, come to us, everybody buys from us. . . ." Dust, shouts and the neighing of horses filled the fair. Earthenware whistles squeaked. The shafts of carts stuck up everywhere. Staggering along, a young man in a blue shirt torn on the shoulder was tugging at an accordion with all his might: "Hi, Dunya, Dunya, Dunya. . . ."

Artyom unharnessed the horses and unshipped the shafts. Just then a man in a military tunic, wearing a sword on a shoulder-strap, came up to Artyom. The man looked at him and shook his head, Artyom also looked at him and removed his cap.

"I've had you before, you tramp," said a mustachioed man, "this time I'll finish you for sure."

"As you will," answered Artyom.

The mustachioed man took him under the elbow and marched him away. The sly old man who was selling pots looked after them and smiled. Mishka Koryashonok whispered to Nikita in worried tones:

"Run and find your father and tell him a policeman has taken Artyom away to the lock-up. I'll look after the carts."

Nikita made his way out of the crowd and ran across the trampled field of feather-grass towards the horse corrals where he could see his father's carriage in the distance. Father, in a very merry mood, was standing at one of the corrals with his hands in his jacket pockets.

126

Nikita began telling him about what had happened to Artyom but Vasily Nikitievich immediately interrupted him.

"Look at that young grey stallion. What a stallion! Wonderful...."

Three Bashkirians in faded quilted robes and caps with earflaps were running about amongst the horses in the corral trying to catch a lively roan stallion with their lariats. The stallion laid back its ears and showed its teeth and shied; it twisted away from the lariats and ran first into the middle of the drove of horses and then out into the open again. Suddenly the horse dropped on to its knees and crawled under the rails of the corral, lifted the rail with its neck, got out and raced away jauntily towards the open grassy steppe, its mane and tail blowing in the wind. Father stamped his feet in delight.

The Bashkirians, wobbling along on their bandy legs, ran for their saddle-horses, short, shaggy little beasts, leaped lightly into their high saddles, two chasing the fugitive and the third with a lariat, to cut him off. The stallion began twisting and turning in the open field but each time he found himself faced by one of the Bashkirians, howling like an animal. The stallion hesitated and a lariat was immediately thrown over his neck. He tried to twist out of it but the Bashkirians slashed his sides with whips and almost strangled him with the lariat. He staggered and fell. The stallion was brought back to the pen in a lather and trembling. A wrinkled old Bashkirian tumbled out of his saddle like a sack of oats and walked over to Vasily Nikitievich.

"Buy the stallion, Sir."

Father laughed and walked over to another corral. Nikita again began telling him about Artyom.

"What a pity," exclaimed Father, "whatever can I do with that idiot? Here, take these twenty kopeks, buy a roll and some fish and wait for me on the carts.... I've sold Zaremka to Medvedev, I sold her cheaply but without any trouble. Run along. I'll come soon."

127

"Soon," however, turned out to be a long time. The big pale-orange sun was hanging over the very edge of the steppe and a haze of golden dust hung over the fair-ground. The church bells were ringing for vespers. Only then did Father put in an appearance. He wore a confused look on his face.

"Quite by accident I have bought a party of camels," he said without looking Nikita in the eyes, "extremely cheap.... Haven't they sent for the mare yet? Funny. And have you sold many of the apples? Only sixty-five kopeks worth? Funny. So that's that: well, to hell with the apples—I told Medvedev that I'd give him the apples together with the mare.... Let's go and rescue Artyom."

Vasily Nikitievich took Nikita round the shoulders and led him through the already quietening fair-ground, between carts that smelled of hay, tar and grain. Here and there they heard songs sung in high-pitched voices that floated away and disappeared in the steppes. A horse neighed.

"Do you know," Father stopped and his eyes flashed slyly. "I'll be in for it when we get home. Well, it doesn't matter. Tomorrow we'll have a look at a trio of horses, all dapple-greys.... May as well be hanged for a sheep as for a lamb."

ON THE CART

That evening Nikita came back from the threshing on a wagon filled with sweet-smelling wheat straw. The narrow strip of sunset, sad and crimson as it always is in autumn, was dying out over the steppe, over the ancient burial mounds, monuments left by nomad tribes that had passed this way in past ages.

In the twilight the furrows could be seen on the empty harvested fields. Here and there the fire of a ploughmen's camp glowed in the darkness and acrid smoke wafted away from it. The cart squeaked and rocked. Nikita lay on his back with his eyes closed. The whole of his body was pleasantly tired. As he dozed off he remembered what had happened during the day.

...Four pairs of strong mares had walked round and round at the end of the thresher shaft. In the middle, on the tiny seat on the beam sat Mishka Koryashonok, shouting and cracking his whip.

An endless belt ran from the wheel on top of the upright that turned with the beam to the red threshing-machine, as big as a house, whose screens and straw bundlers shook madly. The thresher drum rose and

fell with a howl and a ferocious whine that could be heard all over the steppes—it consumed the sheaves as they were thrown in, driving the straw and the grain into the dusty belly of the machine. Vasily Nikitievich himself had been feeding the machine— he wore close-fitting goggles and leather gauntlets that reached to his elbows, his shirt stuck to his back with perspiration, he was all dusty, his beard was covered in chaff and his mouth was black. The creaky carts came rolling up with more sheaves. A lad ran straddle-legged after the conveyor that brought the straw out of the machine, seized huge armfuls, ran up the plank at a trot and hurled the straw on to the rick. Elderly peasants arranged the straw on the ricks with long wooden pitchforks. The cares, toil and alarms of a whole year were over. The whole day long there had been songs and jokes. Artyom was unloading the sheaves from the carts ready for the thresher and the girls had caught hold of him there between the carts and tickled him—a thing he hated—had rolled him over and stuffed his clothes with chaff. That had been great fun! ...

... Nikita opened his eyes. The wagon swayed and creaked. It was by now quite dark in the steppes. The whole sky was covered with the August constellations. The bottomless abyss of the sky was pulsating as though a breeze had passed over the starry dust. The glittering nebula of the Milky Way spread in the dark sky. To Nikita the wagon was like a cradle in which he floated under the stars gazing calmly at distant worlds.

"It's all mine," he thought, "some day I will get on board a flying ship and fly away." And he began to imagine a flying ship with wings like those of a bat, the black emptiness of the sky and the blue shores of an approaching planet—silver mountains, magic lakes, the silhouettes of castles with figures and clouds floating over the water as they do at sunset.

The cart began to descend the hill. Dogs barked in the distance. A breath of dampness came from the ponds. They entered the yard. A cosy warm light poured out of the windows of the house, out of the dining-room.

DEPARTURE

Autumn came and the earth prepared to rest. The sun rose late, there was no warmth in it, an old sun who no longer had any time left for the earth. The birds flew away. The garden emptied, the leaves fell to the ground. The boat was taken out of the pond and put away in a shed, bottom up.

In the 'mornings the grass was grey with hoar-frost in the places that lay in the shadow of the roof. Across the frost-covered, autumn-green grass the geese made their way to the pond—the geese were fat, they wobbled along looking like snowballs. Twelve village girls were chopping cabbage in a big trough outside the workers' quarters—the sound of their songs and their choppers filled the whole yard. Gnawing a cabbage stalk, Dunyasha ran out from the cellar where they were making butter—she had grown prettier over the autumn and her cheeks were so red that everybody knew she wasn't running to the workers' quarters to gnaw cabbage stalks or joke with the girls but so that the young worker Vasily could see her from the window—he was like her, bursting with health and vigour. Artyom was terribly depressed—he was sitting inside mending horse-collars.

Mamma had already moved into the winter part of the house. The stoves had been heated. Akhilka the hedgehog had been dragging rags and paper under the sideboard and fussing around making himself a nest for his winter sleep. Arkady Ivanovich was whistling to himself in his room. Nikita saw him through the keyhole—Arkady Ivanovich was standing in front of the mirror, holding the end of his beard in his hand and whistling thoughtfully: obviously the man was preparing to get married.

Vasily Nikitievich had sent the carts to Samara with grain and had gone there himself the next day. Before he left there had been a long talk with Mamma. She was awaiting a letter from him.

A week later Vasily Nikitievich wrote:

"I have sold the grain and, just imagine, at a good price, better than Medvedev. The case of the inheritance hasn't budged an inch, as was to be expected. The second alternative, which you objected to so strongly, Sasha dear, is absolutely essential. We must not live apart for another winter. I advise you to leave as soon as possible, for the Gymnasium has already begun. It is only by way of exception that

Nikita will be allowed to take the entrance examination for the second form. Incidentally, I have been offered two beautiful Chinese vases —they'll do for our town apartment: it was only fear of angering you that led me to put off the purchase for the time being."

Mamma did not hesitate very long. Fear of leaving Vasily Nikitievich with a large sum of money on his hands, and more especially the fear that he would purchase Chinese vases that nobody had any earthly use for, compelled Alexandra Leontievna to get ready in three days. The furniture that would be needed in town, the big trunks, barrels of salted stuff and the poultry she loaded on to carts and sent off. She went on ahead in two three-horse carriages with Nikita, Arkady Ivanovich and Vasilisa the cook. It was a dull and windy day. On both sides of the road lay empty harvested and ploughed fields. Mamma took pity on the horses and drove at a jog-trot. They spent a night at the inn in Koldyban. By lunch-time the next day the domes of churches and chimneys of the steam flour-mills appeared over the rim of the flat steppe. Mamma was silent: she did not like towns or town life. Arkady Ivanovich was biting his beard in his impatience. For a long time they drove past stinking soap-works, past timber-yards, drove through a dirty suburb with taverns and grocers' shops and over a wide bridge where young bandits from the suburbs waylaid people at night; then came the gloomy log-built granaries on the steep bank of the Samarka River—the tired horses pulled up the hill and the wheels rattled on a paved road. The cleanly dressed passers-by looked with surprise at the muddy carriages. Nikita began to think that both the carriages were ungainly and funny, that the horses were ill-bred peasants' animals—if they would only leave the main street! A black trotter harnessed to a lacquered gig flew past them.

"Sergei Ivanovich, what are you driving so slowly for, drive faster," said Nikita.

"We'll get there like this, too."

Sergei Ivanovich sat sedately and sternly on his box holding his three horses to a trot. At last they turned into a side street, drove past the fire station where a chubby lad in a Grecian helmet was standing at the gate, and came to a standstill outside a one-storey white house with a cast-iron porch that stretched right across the sidewalk. Vasily Nikitievich's joyful face appeared at a window. He waved his hand, disappeared and a minute later opened the front door himself.

Nikita was the first to run into the house. It was very light in the small empty drawing-room with its white wall-paper, near the wall on the shining varnished floor stood two Chinese vases that looked like water-jugs. At the end of the drawing-room, in an arch with white columns that were reflected in the floor, a girl in a brown dress ap-

peared. Her hands were folded under a white pinafore and her brown boots were also reflected in the polished floor. Her hair was done in a plait and behind her ears, on the back of her head, was a white bow. Her blue eyes had a severe look in them, she was almost frowning. It was Lilya. Nikita stood in the middle of the room, rooted to the floor. No doubt Lilya was looking at him in the same way as the people in the main street had looked at the Sosnovka carriages.

"Did you get my letter?" she asked. Nikita nodded. "Where is it? Give it to me this minute."

Although he had not got the letter with him Nikita began fumbling in his pockets. Lilya looked him straight in the eyes, attentively and angrily.

"I wanted to answer, but—" muttered Nikita.

"Where is it?"

"In my portmanteau."

"If you don't give it to me today everything is over between us. I was very sorry that I wrote to you. Now I have entered the first form at the Gymnasium."

She pressed her lips together and stood on tiptoe. It was only now that Nikita realized that he should have answered Lilya's letter. He swallowed hard, dragged his feet from the polished floor.... Lilya immediately hid her hands under her pinafore again—the tip of her nose rose into the air. She showed her contempt by completely veiling her eyes with her long lashes.

"Forgive me," said Nikita, "I'm awful, awful.... It's been all horses, harvesting, threshing, Mishka Koryashonok...."

He turned red and lowered his head. Lilya did not answer. He felt the same disgust for himself as he felt for cow dung. Just then, however, Anna Apollosovna's voice boomed through the entrance-hall, there was an exchange of greetings and the heavy steps of the coachmen carrying in the luggage could be heard. Lilya whispered angrily and quickly:

"They can see us.... You're impossible. Put on a cheerful look ... perhaps I'll forgive you this time...."

She ran out into the hall. From there her thin voice rang through the empty hollow rooms:

"Good-afternoon, Auntie Sasha, welcome to Samara!"

That's how the first day of the new life began. Instead of the calm, pleasant village ease and freedom there were seven small cheerless rooms and outside the windows heavy carts rattling over the cobbles

134

and people dressed like Verinosov, the Zemstvo doctor at Pestravka, running hurriedly along with a worried air, covering their mouths with their coat collars against the wind that blew paper and dust with it. Bustle, noise and disturbing conversations. Even the time passed differently, it flew. Nikita and Arkady Ivanovich fixed up Nikita's room—arranged the furniture and books and put up curtains. At dusk Victor came straight from the Gymnasium and told him that the fifth-form boys smoked in the lavatories and that their arithmetic teacher had been glued to his chair with gum-arabic. Victor was independent and distracted. He got Nikita to give him his penknife with the twelve blades and went to one of his class-mates—"You don't know him"—to play.

Nikita sat at the window in the twilight. The sunset over the town was the same as it had been in the village but Nikita, like Zheltukhin behind his gauze, felt that he was a prisoner, someone who didn't belong there. Just like Zheltukhin. Arkady Ivanovich came into the room wearing his hat and coat and the clean handkerchief in his hand spread the perfume of toilet water.

"I'm going out, I'll be back by about nine."

"Where are you going?"

"To the place where I am not at present." He guffawed. "Well, brother, and how did Lilya receive you? Bit sharp, wasn't she? Never mind, you'll get over it. Sometimes that's even a good thing, to get rid of some of your rural fat." He turned on his heel and went out. In a single day he had become a completely different man.

In a dream that night Nikita saw himself in a blue uniform with silver buttons standing in front of Lilya and saying sternly:

"Here is your letter, take it."

He almost woke up on these words but again saw himself walking across the mirror-like surface of the floor and saying to Lilya:

"Here is your letter, take it."

Lilya's long eyelashes rose and fell, her independent nose was proud and alien and then suddenly the nose and the whole face ceased to wear that alien look and began to laugh. . . .

He awoke and looked round the room. The strange light of a street lamp lay on the wall. . . . Again Nikita had the same dream. In his waking hours he had never loved that inexplicable girl so much. . . .

The next morning Mamma, Nikita and Arkady Ivanovich went to the Gymnasium and talked with the headmaster, a thin, grey-haired, stern-looking man. A week later Nikita passed the examinations and took his place in the second form.

www.ingramcontent.com/pod-product-compliance
Lightning Source LLC
Chambersburg PA
CBHW050759250626
47155CB00005B/2133